The Body of Jonah Boyd

BY THE SAME AUTHOR

Stories
Family Dancing
A Place I've Never Been
The Marble Quilt
Collected Stories

Novels
The Lost Language of Cranes
Equal Affections
While England Sleeps
The Page Turner
Martin Bauman; or, A Sure Thing

Novellas
Arkansas: Three Novellas

Nonfiction
Florence, A Delicate Case

With Mark Mitchell
Italian Pleasures
In Maremma: Life and a House in Southern Tuscany
The Penguin Book of Gay Short Stories (coeditor)
Pages Passed from Hand to Hand (coeditor)

The Body of Jonah Boyd

A Novel

DAVID LEAVITT

BLOOMSBURY

Published by Bloomsbury Publishing, New York and London
Distributed to the trade by Holtzbrinck Publishers

All papers used by Bloomsbury Publishing are natural, recyclable products
made from wood grown in well-managed forests. The manufacturing
processes conform to the environmental regulations of the country of origin.

The Library of Congress has cataloged the hardcover edition as follows:

Leavitt, David, 1961–
The body of Jonah Boyd : a novel / David Leavitt.
p. cm.
ISBN 1-58234-188-5
1. City and town life—Fiction. 2. Female friendship—Fiction. 3. College
teachers—Fiction. 4. Draft resisters—Fiction. 5. Women musicians—Fiction.
6. Secretaries—Fiction. 7. Mistresses—Fiction. 8. Adultery—Fiction.
I. Title.

PS3562.E2618B64 2004
813'.54—dc22
2003020904

First published in the U.S. in hardcover by Bloomsbury Publishing in 2004
This paperback edition published in 2005

Paperback ISBN 1-58234-503-1
ISBN-13 978-1-58234-503-1

1 3 5 7 9 10 8 6 4 2

Typeset by Hewer Text Ltd, Edinburgh
Printed in the United States of America by Quebecor World Fairfield

743 Cooksey Lane

One

EVERY THANKSGIVING, THE Wrights gave a big dinner to which they invited all the graduate students—the
"strays," Nancy Wright called them—who happened to be
marooned in Wellspring over the holiday. Glenn Turner was
usually one of these, as was Phil Perry (later to cause such
grief and uproar), and a shadowy girl with bangs in a plaid
skirt whose name, for the moment, escapes me. Also me. My
name is Judith "Denny" Denham, and I was unique among
the strays in that I wasn't any kind of graduate student. I
was Ernest Wright's secretary in the psych department. Since
the Thanksgiving about which I am writing—1969—thirty
years have passed, which is as many years as I had then been
alive.

In Wellspring, California, many of the street names combine
the front and back ends of different states. Calibraska Avenue
is the main shopping thoroughfare, rising at a steady eastward
incline from the university and then crossing under the 420
freeway to Springwell, where I lived, where most of the
secretaries lived. Springwell is Wellspring's service entrance,
its mirror twin; it is where you go for the best Mexican food,
or to visit your children by a woman you have long since
abandoned; it is the wrong side of a freeway the chief function

of which, I often suspect, is to give people something to live on the *right* side of.

Florizona Avenue, where the Wrights lived, is on the university side of the freeway—the right side. It begins its brief, three-block trajectory as a sharp left turn off Minnetucky Road, then winds upward amid rows of capacious houses, most of them two-story, shingled or stucco, with somersaulting lawns and old oaks—and then, just at its point of greatest glory, where the view opens up to reveal all of Wellspring, the university with its tiled roofs, and the arroyo, and on sunny days, in the remote distance, the Pacific, it comes to an abrupt end at Washaho Avenue, the name of which has for generations been the subject of crude undergraduate jokes. Today, due to the university's peculiar charter, this neighborhood remains the exclusive domain of tenured professors and senior administrators, even as the rest of Wellspring has been colonized by movie people and software engineers from the "campuses" of the tech firms that have sprung up of late in the hills, as if in parody of the real campus to which the town owes its name. The reigning provost, Ira Weiss, is at 304, formerly the Webb house, while at 310, where Ken Longabaugh from Math once lived with his wife, Hettie, there's a Russian biologist named Federov. Francine Chambers from History has replaced Jim Heatherly from Geology at 307. 305 still belongs to Sam and Bertha Boxer—"the bizarre Boxers," as we used to call them, Sam long retired from the Engineering department and their yard more dilapidated than ever.

As for the Wrights' house—302—after Nancy Wright died in 1981, it went through three more owners, the price doubling with each resale, until Ben Wright, by then a famous novelist, managed at long last to buy it back in the late nineties. He lived there until his own death last spring.

I remember that when I first started working at Wellspring, I used to sometimes take Florizona Avenue on my way home from the office, just so that I could admire, for a moment, its easy affluence, the fruit trees and rose gardens and winding stone paths. After school, if it wasn't raining, there would be children in the street, playing Capture the Flag or Red Rover, though Ben Wright was rarely among them. His allergies kept him indoors. In those days I thought the name "Florizona" exotic and colorful; it brought to mind some tropical tree, a palm or a banyan, growing out of hot sand, in a landscape as crooked and severe as the one through which the Road Runner chases the coyote.

Ernest Wright was an authority on Freud, and also maintained a small private practice as a psychoanalyst. Although he had been born in St. Louis, where he had met and married Nancy, his ancestry was Eastern European, his parents having emigrated from Poland around the turn of the century and adopted the name "Wright" in honor of the brothers who made the first successful airplane flight. (His father had ambitions to be a pilot.) For much of his professional life, Ernest taught at Bradford College in Bradford, New Hampshire. The Wrights only moved to Wellspring in 1964, two years before I went to work as his secretary.

They had three children: Mark, Daphne, and Ben. In 1969, Mark was twenty and living in Vancouver. That summer, he had fled over the Canadian border to avoid the military draft. His draft number was four. Daphne was seventeen in 1969, and in the throes of her first real love affair, with Glenn Turner, who was her father's protégé. (This had to be kept

3

secret from Ernest, who wouldn't have approved.) In those years, she and her mother were waging a constant war the chief purpose of which, or so it seemed to me, was to allow them to collapse, at battle's end, into a cozy mess of tears, hugs, and chocolate ice cream. To prolong the ordeal of fighting in order to intensify the pleasure of making up—this was classic Wright behavior, and worthy of just the sort of Freudian analysis that Ernest was so skilled at doling out in every context except that of his own family.

Ben was the youngest—fifteen in 1969. He wrote poetry, and was a picky eater. At Thanksgiving dinners, if any one of the foods on his plate touched any other—if the peas touched the turkey or the gravy got onto the marshmallow-crusted sweet potato casserole—he would refuse to eat altogether. His eating habits were a source of great distress for Nancy, who seemed incapable of getting her son's meals arranged properly, and eventually had to buy him a special plate divided into sections to keep him from starving himself.

My friendship with Nancy was in certain crucial ways remote from my relationship with her husband. Having heard that I could play the piano, she had asked me to be her four-hand partner. And though, as a four-hand partner, I didn't prove to be very good—I was inclined to play wrong notes or fall out of step with her scrupulous metronome—still, she kept at it with me, and kept inviting me to Thanksgiving dinners, in part, I think, because I could be counted on to make gravy without lumps, as my mother had taught me, and to take on the more onerous of the cooking chores, the ones Daphne disdained, such as chopping the carrots. Our friendship, which lasted almost fifteen years, was fractious and sometimes maudlin. Nancy resented me for not playing the piano as well as Anne Armstrong, her four-hand partner and best friend from Bradford; I resented Nancy for treating me as an unpaid servant, inviting me to the parties and faculty wives teas that she sometimes hosted and then expecting me to wash the dishes or pour the coffee. And yet I also adored her, and craved the maternal solicitude she dispensed, as I had lost my own mother when I was fourteen. And she, if nothing else, seemed to feel that she could talk to me as she could to few others, that I would listen to her complaints and worries without judging her or ignoring her, as Ernest was wont to do. Friendships between women are often like that, made up of blame and neediness in equal portions.

Nineteen sixty-nine was the third Thanksgiving that I spent with the Wrights—an exceptional Thanksgiving, in that Mark, for the first time, was absent (Nancy wept about it), while two honored guests were to be in attendance: the novelist Jonah Boyd and his new wife, the former Anne Armstrong, Nancy's erstwhile four-hand partner and best friend from Bradford.

It was difficult to imagine Nancy Wright away from her house. It seemed to be a part of her, her very soul bound up with its beams and plaster. Yet the first time she walked into the kitchen, she sat down on her suitcase and wept.

This was a famous story, one she told many times. "Well, you know that before we came to Wellspring, we lived in Bradford," she'd begin. "We'd already been there a dozen years, Ernest had tenure, Mark and Daphne were in school with kids they'd known their whole lives. Also, we'd just moved into our dream house—I mean that literally, because I saw the house in a dream. I woke up and drew it before the image faded, and gave the drawing to the architect, and that was the house he built, more or less. It was three stories, but you entered on the middle story. One staircase went down, to the family room and the kids' bedrooms. The other went up, to our bedroom and Ernest's study. We had a fountain in the front and glass all around the front door—gorgeous, except that the birds couldn't tell that it was glass. I'd be practicing Mozart on the piano, when suddenly there'd be this thwacking noise, and a bird body would drop to the ground. Dead. Horrible.

"After we built that house, I hoped we'd stay there the rest of our lives. And why not? You took settlement more for granted in those days. But then Ernest got the offer from Wellspring, and it was that proverbial 'offer you can't refuse.' He asked me if I minded. He said that if I minded, of course he'd turn down the offer. I said that I minded, and he called to accept.

"We put the house in Bradford on the market. The kids were miserable. They didn't want to leave their friends. And then at the end of the summer, we made what my best pal Anne Armstrong liked to call 'the great migration'—as if we were crossing the prairie in a covered wagon! In fact, Ernest went first—he drove—and then a couple of weeks later, I flew out with the kids. He didn't ask my opinion about the house on Florizona Avenue. He just called me up one day and announced that he'd bought it. Case closed. Never even bothered to send me a photograph.

"I remember that when we arrived at the airport, he had a new car waiting for us, a Ford Falcon station wagon with a red interior, which I guess was supposed to make the kids feel better. Even though we were booked to stay at a motel for a couple of nights, I made him drive us straight to the new house. Today it may be hard for you to envision, because of course we've done so much redecorating since then, and put in the pool, and landscaped, but the first time I saw it, the house was a total wreck. The window frames were rotting. There were birds' nests between the screens and the windows, and all the gutters were clogged with pine needles.

"We didn't go in through the front door. We went up the back staircase—there was a hole in one of the treads—and then Ernest put the key in the door, which wouldn't budge because the lock was rusty. So we all just stood there in the cold, until finally he got it open and let us inside. 'Ta-da,' he said, and I just stared. The kitchen floor was this hideous linoleum, printed to look like terrazzo. There was no refrigerator, just a gaping hole where a refrigerator ought to be. The cabinets were made of this awful old rusty metal, painted red. You see, before he'd signed the papers, Ernest had let the contractor convince him that all the renovation work, or at least most of it, could be finished by the time we arrived. You know how contractors are, they'll say anything to get a job—and you know how gullible Ernest can be! As if that much work could be done in such a short time! Visionary, but no common sense. And so we stood there in the middle of the wreckage, the kids flying around like moths, and Ernest says, 'So what do you think?' And when I don't answer, he says, 'It'll be gorgeous once it's finished.' And that's when I sit down on my suitcase and start to cry.

"Whenever I tell people this story, I know they think I'm exaggerating, because—well, the house turned out to be so wonderful, didn't it, and now we've had so many Thanksgiving dinners here, and beginning-of-semester cocktail parties, and pool parties? I think back to the house in Bradford, and it's hard to imagine I ever assumed we'd always live there. You know, I really believe that for some of us, there is a house that is a kind of destiny, a place that, once you arrive there, you say, 'Yes, this is where I belong,' and you stay. That's what this house is for me. And yet I was forty-four years old before I even saw it. I'd lived in six houses already, including my parents' house. All of which just goes to prove that you should never try to second-guess the future."

Perhaps at this point both the house and Nancy ought to be described. The house dated from the early 1920s and had begun life as a country cottage, back in the days when this part of California was still country. At first it had consisted of a simple shingled rectangle, a dash, but then each successive owner had added a wing, so that over the course of decades, the dash became a sideways T, then a lowercase h, then a capital H—the shape it bore when Ernest Wright bought it.

It had some wonderful, odd features. Just to the left stood an old-fashioned garage, a separate building with a weather vane and its own attic, which Ernest later made over into the office where he saw his patients. In the backyard, near the pool, there was a sloped, grass-lined depression where an earlier pool had been dug in the twenties and then abandoned, victim of the stock market crash. Later, an intermediate owner had tried to make a virtue of this strange declivity by building a turreted barbecue pit at the deep end, and lining the sides with brick benches. Because the chimney smoked, no one used it—yet what a wonderful place it was to run, and turn somersaults, and imagine yourself the protector of a medieval keep in the midst of battle! Dame Carcas throwing the pig over the wall of Carcassone . . . I never played such games, only fantasized

8

about having played them, when I pretended that I had grown up in that house.

What else? The house was shingled, and during most of the years I knew it, painted red. It was one story, but because the lot sloped down, its rear end rose up over the garden. Although the brick path from Florizona Avenue descended to a veranda and a rather grand front door inlaid with stained glass, no one in the family ever entered that way. *That* door was used only by party guests and delivery men; the Wrights themselves went in through the back, by means of that rickety wooden staircase that led from the garage to the kitchen, which was big, with a Saarinen tulip table, a faux-brick vinyl floor (to replace the old linoleum), and oak cabinets painted robin's egg blue. The kitchen was really the hub of that house. It was here that the Wrights ate their weekday dinners, and that the children did their homework, and that Nancy fumed and fretted as she polished the copper bottoms of her Revereware. In that kitchen, on a little television next to the sink, we watched the kidnapping of Patty Hearst and the impeachment of Nixon, Nancy swearing like a sailor each time Henry Kissinger's face appeared and turning down the volume because, she said, that man was the devil incarnate, and she could not bear even the sound of his voice.

The kitchen opened up onto the dining room, which was rectangular, with shag carpeting in three shades of gold, and a chair rail of white beadboard that ran to about four and a half feet above the floor and ran the length of the walls. This chair rail supported a shelf that over the fireplace widened into a mantel and then narrowed again as it continued its journey around the room. Nancy used it to display mementos and knickknacks, everything from a taxidermied piranha to a clay impression of Mark's hand from when he was in kindergarten. On the first day of December, though, all of this decorative rubbish would be cleared away to make room for the onslaught of Christmas cards that the Wrights received annually, as many from psychoanalytic institutes, colleagues, and former patients of Ernest's as from relatives and friends. In those volatile years, it was fashionable to write a Christmas letter or verse and have it printed on the card along with a photograph of the sender's family, and sometimes these works had an unintended edge of heartbreak:

> Jane and Allen's twelfth anniversary
> Was celebrated with divorce.
> The party, though, was only cursory,
> The marriage having run its course.

To the right of the fireplace, a curved archway led into the living room, the least used room in the house, with its Danish modern leather chairs, one of which the cat, Dora, had peed on the day it had been delivered; the stain was still there a dozen years later. Here, too, was the piano, a matte black 1920 Knabe with beautifully fluted legs. Nancy had bought it "for a song" (her joke) at an estate sale. And then—the bar connecting the two parts of the H—there was the front hall, with the stained-glass door that nobody used, and off of that a sort of family room that had been Ernest's study before he'd moved into the attic above the garage, but which Nancy still called the study, and where you would usually find Little Hans, the family schnauzer, asleep on a leather rocking chair. (Little Hans, Dora—everything in that house was a Freud joke.) It was in the study as well that Ernest kept his collection of toy airplanes, a rare foray into sentimentality for him, gathered mostly to honor the memory of his father, who had dreamed of flight since boyhood but had himself flown only once, near the very end of his life, on a commuter plane that carried him from St. Louis to Chicago to visit a heart specialist.

On the other side of the front hall was the bedroom wing. There were four bedrooms, the largest Nancy and Ernest's, the smallest Ben's. Mark's room Ernest had had made over into a library almost as soon as his son had left for Vancouver. Daphne's had a queen-size bed and therefore did double duty as the guest room on those rare occasions when there were overnight guests. A corner bathroom with two entrances connected this room to Ben's. He often complained that his sister woke him up in the small hours with her loud and frequent peeing. About these rooms I can tell you less than I can about the others, because I very rarely had occasion to go into them.

Outside, in addition to the barbecue pit, there was a good-size swimming pool that the Wrights themselves had had built, and in which Nancy swam a rigorous twenty laps daily, even in bad weather. There was also a camellia garden, and a vegetable garden, and a koi pond with no koi; one winter, preparatory to repairing a leak, Ernest had drained it and put the koi into a barrel, from which they'd been stolen, over the course of a single night, by a family of raccoons. After that he gave up on koi, and filled the pond with impatiens—another oddity, the fish pond/flower bed, in that yard where nothing was what it had been meant to be.

As for Nancy—well, if the barbecue pit was Carcassone, *she* was Dame Carcas: tall, with a stately bearing. Tight curls,

11

black going to gray, helmeted her head. She had a snub nose. Her eyes were the color of raisins. I remember that in those years, as was the fashion, she often dressed in flowing saris, muumuus patterned with exotic flowers, the sort of dresses that transform fat women into shapeless balls but lend to statuesque women like Nancy an even more imperious, aristocratic aspect. Her breasts protruded, one might say, with pride, they were like the buttresses of a cathedral. Whether she was smoking a cigarette on the porch, or feeding the cat, or overseeing the preparation of the Thanksgiving turkey, she radiated the slightly weary, slightly burdened grandeur of one of those monarchs whose biographies she was forever reading—Mary, Queen of Scots, Catherine the Great. But more than either of them, Elizabeth I. In her imagination, I fancy she saw herself as the reincarnation of the Virgin Queen.

One peculiarity of home ownership in the neighborhoods immediately surrounding the Wellspring campus is that the university itself owns all the land. When you buy a house, you buy *only* the house; the land will then be leased to you for ninety-nine years at the rate of a dollar a year—*but only on the condition that you are a tenured professor or senior administrator at the university*. And though a spouse can inherit a lease, it can be passed on to a child only in the unlikely circumstance that the child, too, is a tenured professor or senior administrator at the university—a rule that enraged Nancy, who had a mystic feeling for her home, and wanted it to remain in the family. What plots were hatched in the seventies to get Daphne—now a psychologist—a position at the student health center! All to no avail. Ernest was killed, and Nancy died, and the house passed out of the family's hands, until Ben, rather remarkably, reclaimed it.

12

To understand how this odd provision came into being (and it really is the heart of the story), you need to know something about Wellspring's history. The university was chartered in 1910, when cattle baron and theosophy devotee Josiah Reddicliffe sectioned off ten thousand acres of hilly farmland for the purposes of founding a college that would serve as "a wellspring of knowledge and hope forever more." The "forever more" is key: Although the charter invested the board of trustees with the power to decide just how to *use* the land, it stipulated that not even an acre of it could be sold. In its early years, Wellspring was isolated, an "Eden of learning" amid the arroyos and swaying grasses. And this was just how Josiah Reddicliffe wanted it: He had a vision of sturdy young males going out to round up cattle after a few hours spent reading Pliny the Elder. But then a few merchants and bankers, doctors and lawyers, opened shops and practices on the fringes of the campus. In 1920, the town of Wellspring was officially incorporated. Four years later, chiefly to appease certain members of the faculty who were getting weary of the commute from Pasadena, the board of trustees came up with the land lease scheme that obtains to the present day. These professors built the first houses on Florizona Avenue, including the one Nancy Wright was so determined to keep for her children.

Why did she care so much? Ernest certainly didn't. Indeed, one afternoon a few months before his death, he came home and announced quite casually that he'd just put the house on the market, and put a down payment on a new condominium on Oklakota Road. Nancy's outrage, he later said, baffled him. Why should they go on rattling around in such a big house, he argued, especially now that he was retiring, and Daphne and Mark were on their own, and Ben was about to start college? He was not the sort of man to understand the mysterious sensibilities that yoke some people to their homes. "I hardly even notice where I live," he told me once. "Rooms, furniture. Intelligent people don't care about these things." Still, on this occasion at least, Nancy must have prevailed— whether through threats or pleading or bargaining, I shall never know, the secrets of that bedroom having died with its occupants—for a few days later, he withdrew the offer on the condominium, and stopped the sale of the house.

It was after he was killed, and she was diagnosed with a brain tumor, that Nancy began in earnest her campaign to keep the house. In this she was joined by Daphne and Ben, both of whom had by then moved back home, and who shared her obsession. Right out of college, Daphne had married Glenn Turner—principally, I think, because Glenn now had a position as an assistant professor at Wellspring, and there- fore a shot at being able to buy the house. But then Glenn was turned down for tenure, and Daphne left him, landing on her mother's doorstep with two small children in tow. Likewise Ben, for somewhat more obscure reasons, decided to return from New York to the family fold. The three of them, along with the two grandchildren, were living together in the house (only Mark—married now, and a lawyer in Toronto—had achieved any degree of independence) when Nancy arranged her famous meeting with the provost, the meeting at which he tried to explain to her, as calmly as possible, the university's position, the consensus that, were the rule in question ever to be changed, or an exception made, within a matter of years, nearly every house on Florizona Avenue would belong to the child of a professor, and there would be nowhere for the professors themselves to live. Worse, some of those children might decide to try to profit from the situation by selling their houses to "outsiders" of the sort who were even then colonizing the rest of the community. Prices would rise to such a level that no faculty member could *afford* to live on Florizona Avenue—an argument against which, like all the others, she stopped her ears. Her opinion was fixed and passionate: That house, for her, was more than a house; it was a spiritual inheritance, her children's birthright. As she left the provost's office, she swore that she would never give up. If need be, she would die fighting.

After that she really got going. First she organized a petition drive, soliciting all her neighbors for support. Then she barraged the board of trustees with letters. Then she persuaded a reporter from the *Wellspring Sentinel* to do a story "exposing" a rule little known outside the university. Lastly, she threatened the administration with a lawsuit—all without success. The petition drive yielded only a few dozen signatures, the board of trustees rejected her arguments, the article in the *Sentinel* was buried near the back page, the lawsuit never got off the ground. By the time Nancy died, all her efforts had been exhausted—and yet, even in her final delirium, she could speak of little else besides the house. To comfort her, Ben lied. He told her that at the eleventh hour, the provost had given in, agreeing that the Wright children could take over the land lease. And she accepted what he told her, or at least pretended to, and seemed to die in peace. Teary-eyed yet stoic, Ben and Daphne now organized the estate sale during which much of their parents' worldly chattel was sold and hauled off, including the Danish modern leather chair with the cat pee on it, and the piano, and the stuffed piranha. Dora was dead. I took Little Hans, who lived with me until his own death a few years later. Two law professors—a married couple—bought the house, and Ben and Daphne, each bearing a third of the considerable profits, went their separate ways. For years I didn't hear from them. I didn't know that they were still plotting. I didn't know that, especially for Ben, the reclaiming of that house, the fulfillment of that final lie at his mother's deathbed, had become the driving ambition of a frustrated and unhappy life.

Two

NANCY WRIGHT "FOUND" me, as she found so many of her friends, at the hairdresser's. This was in November 1967. I suppose I should say something more about what I was like at that time. I was twenty-eight, and had been working at Wellspring for just over a year. I was fat, with freckled, vigorous cheeks, and most of the time I wore men's Oxford shirts and denim skirts with elasticized waistbands. I still do. Perhaps because of this, most people assume me to be a sexless spinster, or short of that a lesbian, when in fact I have always had a fairly easy time attracting men. Wives be warned: It is not necessarily the glamorous woman, the woman with the pronounced cheekbones and the red hair piled loosely atop her head, who is the femme fatale. On the contrary, the homely secretary may pose a graver threat to your domestic security. For there is often a great disparity between what men actually want and what they feel, for the sake of appearances, they should pretend to want. Thus, even within the deceptive realm of infidelity, one encounters secondary levels of deception. One of the married men with whom I had an affair, when his wife found a love letter he had written to me, insisted that it was for another woman—a more conventionally "pretty" woman—that the missive was meant. Others were glad to sleep with me, but would not be seen with me at restaurants. This attitude probably would have caused me greater offense had it not fit so well my need for privacy and independence. I was a creature too prone to passionate excess to thrive within the conjugal yoke. Affairs with married men better suited my character and disposition. The married men appreciated that I had no wish to interfere with their domestic stability. I appreciated that they were less likely to importune, to demand total loyalty, than would a conventional suitor. It was a system that worked well through a number of long affairs, including one with Ernest Wright.

And why, I now find myself trying to recall, had I gone to the hairdresser's in the first place? I wasn't in the habit of doing so—even then, I preferred to keep my hair short and to the point—only that week one of the other secretaries in my department must have put it into my head that I ought to "do" something with my hair, such as have it set. And so that Saturday, more to appease a sense of youthful insecurity than from any genuine enthusiasm, I went to Minnie's Beauty Salon on Calibraska Avenue. I endured the ordeal of having my hair washed, cut, and then rolled with curlers, after which I was put to roost under one of the old-fashioned, kettle-shaped dryers. Next to me Nancy knitted. We had only met once before, at a department function.

"Hello," she said. "Do you play piano?"

I thought I'd misheard her. "Excuse me?" I asked.

"Oh, it's you," she said. "Sorry, I didn't recognize you under there. How are things going?"

"Oh, hello, Mrs. Wright! Fine, thank you."

"I hope Ernest hasn't terrorized you too much."

"No, not at all."

"I'm only asking about the piano because I'm looking for a four-hand partner. *Do* you play?"

"Badly," I admitted.

"Good, that's just how I play," she said, and dropped a stitch.

Ben was with her. I don't know why. He must have been thirteen at the time. He was sitting near the window, scowling at Robert Graves's *Greek Myths*. "Ben, say hello to Daddy's new secretary, Miss Denham," Nancy shouted.

Ben mumbled something.

"What was that?" Nancy called, so that people turned. "E-nun-ci-ate."

"Pleased to meet you," Ben screamed.

"No need to shout."

"It's not my fault that you can't hear under that thing."

He returned to his book. In those days there was still an old-fashioned drugstore on Calibraska Avenue, with a lunch counter. Those customers who happened to have appointments at Minnie's over the lunch hour made it their habit to order in cheeseburgers, BLTs, and the like, and eat them under the dryers. Now a delivery boy came through the door, bearing bags of food, and Minnie called out our orders.

"Chicken salad?"

Ben and I raised our hands simultaneously and were each handed a sandwich in wax paper. Already addled by Nancy's interrogation, I unwrapped mine without ceremony and started gobbling.

Suddenly Ben put his sandwich down.

"What is it?" his mother asked.

"It's not on toast," Ben said.

"Well, the drugstore must have forgotten," Nancy said. "These things happen."

"But I ordered it on toast."

"Now Ben—"

"*She* has my sandwich!" he cried, pointing at me. I stopped chewing. And it was true; on closer examination, I saw that my sandwich *was* toasted. Clearly Minnie had mixed up our orders.

"Oh, I'm sorry," I said. "Here"—and realized that I had already eaten half.

What I didn't know—what I wouldn't learn until a few months later—was that among the many food phobias from which Ben suffered at the time was an irrational aversion to untoasted bread; he simply refused to eat untoasted bread, which he claimed was "germy." Nor was he remotely gracious during the fretful parrying that followed. I apologized; he sulked. Despite his mother's remonstrances, he would neither accept the remaining half of my sandwich, nor allow a new one to be ordered for him. "I'm so sorry," Nancy said. "Go ahead and finish your lunch." But of course mortification and pride forbade me from taking so much as a bite. Nancy couldn't finish her grilled cheese, either. I wondered if I'd have to quit my job, or ask to be transferred to a different department.

Afterwards, she tried to make it up to me. "He's a sensitive boy," she said. "He writes poetry."

"How nice," I answered. In truth, I was thinking only that as soon as I could decently ask to be unplugged from the dryer, I would get out of Minnie's, never to return. Yet Nancy was not about to let me off so easily; she could be assaultive in her generosity, especially if she felt that she had a debt to repay. "Let's do play together," she urged. "You could come over on Saturdays, when you're off work. I'll make lunch afterward. Where are you from, by the way?"

"North Florida."

"Do you live alone? Are you going home for Thanksgiving? Come for Thanksgiving."

"But—"

"Unless you have other plans. Are you going back East? To your family?"

I didn't feel like explaining that I had no family, so I just said, "No."

"Then it's settled." She wrote the address down on one of Minnie's business cards. "Oh, and if you come early, we can try some four-hand. Too-da-loo."

They left. I thought that I would wait a few days and then call to say I couldn't come; that I had "forgotten" a previous invitation. But the next day at work, Ernest said, "So happy you'll be coming to Thanksgiving. Nancy told me about running into you, and she's tickled pink." (Such locutions as "tickled pink" often slipped through the veneer of old-world severity that he affected, recalling his Midwestern childhood.)

"Dr. Wright," I said, "really, it's very sweet of you, but I wouldn't want you to feel— from a sense of duty—"

"Do you often feel people ask you places from a sense of duty?"

"Yes. No."

"Which one?"

"I don't know."

"Well, think about it," he said. "And perhaps we can talk about it more on Thanksgiving, hmm?"

Thanksgiving was the following Thursday. Per Nancy's instructions, at eleven o'clock in the morning I made my way down the brick path to the front door, and rang the bell.

21

Daphne let me in. She was in her nightgown. Her long blond hair—which she rarely bothered to comb—gave her a look of careless prettiness, or pretty carelessness. "Mom, someone's here," she said through a yawn. "Come in." And she led me through to the kitchen.

From the stove, Nancy waved a baster in greeting. A cigarette smoldered in an ashtray next to a large pan filled with breadcrumb stuffing. There was a festive, roasting smell. I had dressed carefully—and all wrong, I saw now—in a dark blue suit and cream-colored blouse with a frilly collar: the outfit I had worn when I had gone to interview for my job. Nancy, by contrast, was wearing a muumuu patterned with wild green flowers that looked like they might bite your hand off, and orange flames shooting forth toward jagged peaks: the very embodiment of Florizona.

On subsequent Thanksgivings, the moment I arrived, Nancy would draft me into chopping something. This time, however, having accepted the bottle of wine I had brought, she instructed Daphne to "keep an eye on the bird," and took me off on a tour of the house. In terms of detail, I absorbed very little that first visit, though I did notice the toy airplanes, and the piano, and that the furniture in the living room was strikingly "modern." Nancy introduced me again to Ben, and for the first time to Mark, who was now a sophomore at Wellspring, with a bony, brooding face and a unibrow. They were sitting on the study sofa, thumbing through a book of *Krazy Kat* cartoons. By way of greeting, Mark looked up and gave me one of those frowns that can be so much more compelling and attractive than a smile. His very straight brown hair was parted in the middle and cut severely just below the ears, while Ben had shaggy, rather dry hair,

paler than his brother's, and inclined to wave. Even so, he too
had parted it in the middle. Like Mark, he had his left leg
crossed manfully over his right, ankle on knee. They wore
more or less identical outfits—pale Oxford shirts and flared
jeans—but because Ben's legs were so long in relation to his
torso, his didn't seem to hang on him properly. The jeans
rode up, revealing a band of pale flesh just above the sock
line.

We finished up in the bedroom wing. "I won't subject you
to Daphne's chaos," Nancy said, bypassing one closed door
and opening another to reveal the master bedroom, which
was utterly pristine, the enormous bed made up for the
occasion with the "dress" bedspread, tailored from heavy
slub linen. From here we walked out onto the back porch,
which ran the whole length of the house and gave onto a
vista of old oaks, red-leafed Japanese maples, and a few
exotic fruit trees, including a guava. A very green lawn
swept down to the pool, which had been built parallel to
the barbecue pit; beyond that I could make out just the edge
of the former koi pond, as well as some exuberant rose
bushes. For the first but by no means the last time she told
me the story of how she and Ernest had come to acquire the
house.

There was a moment of spectacular quiet in which all you
could hear was the remote trilling of a lark. "It's very beautiful," I said—ineptly, I thought—and Nancy, her breast rising
with emotion, gave me a smile to suggest regal forbearance:
noblesse oblige.

"I shall never live anywhere else," she said. "When they take
me out of here, it'll be feet first in a pine box." Then she lit a
cigarette. "Well, we'd better be getting back to the kitchen,

shouldn't we?" And she walked me across the porch to the back door.

The kitchen was empty. "Oh, where is Daphne?" Nancy inquired of no one, and ran to open the oven. In those years supermarket turkeys almost always came with a little built-in thermometer that popped up when the meat reached a certain temperature; fortunately, we now discovered, the device remained unejaculated, which meant that even though Daphne had fallen down on the job, the meal's ruination was not imminent.

In fact, Daphne was in her room. Through the locked door, Nancy shouted, "Daph! What are you doing? I asked you to keep an eye on the turkey! Do I have to do everything myself around here? And while you're in there, do something with your hair. It looks like a rat's nest."

We returned to the living room, where she sat me down at the piano. "Let's start with this," she said, arranging some music on the desk. "It's a baby transcription of Beethoven's Eighth Symphony."

The truth was, it had been several years since I'd sat in front of a piano. All through elementary school and high school, in our little town in Florida, my sister and I had taken lessons from Miss Busby, who lived with her own sister in the country and was paralyzed from the waist down. Her house was built from heart pine and had what was known as a "dog trot," a long corridor through which a cooling breeze blew even on the hottest summer afternoons. But now it was almost a decade since I'd left Miss Busby, and my sister, and our little town. I'd followed a boyfriend to California, where he'd married someone else.

"Be patient with me," I said, cracking my fingers. "I may be rusty."

"Don't do that," Nancy said. "It'll bring on arthritis."

"I know. I shouldn't. I won't."

"Now—one, two, three—" And we began.

That day we played for almost an hour. I was dreadful, though not as dreadful as I'd feared I'd be. And Nancy, to her credit, was patient with me, offering gentle pointers when I made a mistake, or lost my way. "Trust me, it'll sound better next week," she said as we finished, then closed the music desk, after which we returned to the kitchen, where Daphne, Mark, and Ben were playing Scrabble at the tulip table. This was one Thanksgiving tradition; another, more obscure in origin, was to play Edith Piaf records on the Harmon-Kardon stereo.

It all rather overwhelmed me. Until then, I had only experienced family life from a great remove—on television, or at the house of a great aunt in Tallahassee, to which my sister and I were sometimes invited out of pity in the years after our father ran away and our mother died. And now here I stood, an old maid in an inappropriately formal suit, while Edith Piaf sang "*Je ne regrette rien*," and teenagers laughed, and from the upper of the two wall ovens there wafted a smell of meat and onions and sage, and from the lower one a smell of nutmeg and pumpkin. Ernest came in, smoking a pipe. Most of the morning he'd been in his office over the garage. He was wearing a bow tie. With him was Glenn Turner, who had just finished his Ph.D. He too was smoking a pipe; he too was wearing a bow tie.

"You look like twins," I said—the first casual remark I'd made all day. It brought a spurt of laughter from Daphne.

The rest of that day is a blur of yearning and dread: yearning to have had a different life, to have been Daphne, and grown up in that house; dread of the moment when politeness would compel me to make my farewells, and retreat to my dreary little apartment in Springwell. I volunteered to make the gravy, and to my surprise, my offer was accepted. Nancy complimented me on its smoothness. Despite being so skinny, Phil Perry, then already in his third year in the psych department, ate twice as much as anyone else, and was congratulated for it. The girl with the bangs in the plaid skirt told a long, boring story about her father losing his dog.

As for Ernest—he got drunk, and while everyone else was gathering in the living room for coffee, he cornered me in the kitchen and tried to kiss me. This didn't surprise me. In those years, men took what opportunities they could get.

"Such a pretty little thing," he said, nuzzling my ear.

"Dr. Wright, please!" I said—more because it was what I thought I *should* say than because I objected, or even cared particularly.

"When you typed that article for me last week, what did you think? You know the one I mean—"

"I just type. I think about typing."

"Say the title."

" 'Female Masturbation and the Electra Complex.' "

"Do you get excited when you read those words? 'Female masturbation'? Say it again. Please."

Ben came in, and we separated. I don't know if he saw us. He gave his father a murderous stare.

Straightening my skirt, I returned to the living room. Ernest and Ben followed. Later, I drove back to my apartment in my new Dodge Dart. I had a lot to think about: not merely

Ernest's come-on, but Nancy's weird avidity to win me as a friend. Why were they so interested in me? I was just a secretary. True, in other arenas of my life, I could conduct myself with confidence and grace, but back in those early days, interacting with members of the faculty made me shy. After all, these people had doctorates from grand universities—while I had only a high school diploma. Later, I would cease to be so easily impressed—I would learn that Ph.D.'s from Harvard could be blithering idiots, just as secretaries could be geniuses—but back then I was still naïve. And so as I opened the door to my apartment, I found myself not only reviewing the events of the evening, but wondering whether behind the kindness the Wrights had shown me there might not lie some nefarious motive; might I perhaps have been the subject of some psychological experiment, my every action and reaction recorded, analyzed, assessed? Hidden cameras, Dictaphones in the potted plants, Glenn and Phil taking notes: Lying in bed that night, I let paranoia get the better of me. Probably the Wrights simply liked me, I reminded myself. Or felt sorry for me. I would have to get to know them better before I could say for certain.

Monday I was back at the office. I worried that Ernest might make some reference to our clinch in the kitchen, but he acted as if nothing had happened. "So I'll be seeing you on Saturday mornings from now on?" he asked.

"If you're home," I said.

He was home. While Nancy and I played, he puttered around in the study, ostensibly fixing the stereo and alerting us every time one of us hit a wrong note, which was often. This time Nancy was less patient. As I would soon learn, the role into which she had conscripted me was one for which several professors' wives had already auditioned and been turned down. Why I succeeded where they failed I still don't know. Perhaps I simply buckled under more willingly to her domination; or perhaps she really did love me in a way she loved few others. Certainly in those early days of our friendship it seemed that her wish was to nurture and cultivate me, to bring me along in the world as if I were another daughter of that house. Nor can it be denied that each week she treated me more like Daphne. "Careful, Denny!" she'd shout, if I accidentally turned two pages at once; or if I had trouble with octaves—"It's so simple, just look!" she'd say, and grab hold of my hands, smashing them into position against the keys. "I see now," I'd say, and we'd try again, and again I'd fall apart.

"You're just not concentrating. I never had these problems with Anne. We played so perfectly together, the harmonies—they were almost magical."

"You must miss her."

"We were the same size, we could wear the same clothes."

"What did you talk about while you played?"

"Husbands. Things."

There was no way I could have gotten into Nancy's clothes. Nor could I talk with her about husbands, as I had none.

As the weeks passed, more and more Anne became the principal topic of our conversations: Anne and, more specifically, my failure to live up to Anne in almost every regard. In Bradford, she and Nancy had played five days a week—Mozart, some Brahms waltzes, a stab at Schubert's "Grand Duo." Because I worked, I could only manage Saturday mornings—a source of some annoyance to Nancy, though clearly not enough to induce her to go off in search of a partner with more time on her hands. Soon I began to catch on that my function was not, in fact, to improve. My function was to exalt, by my very incompetence, the true friend, Anne, swindled away by distance and Ernest's ambitions. The race was fixed. By losing, I fulfilled my part of the bargain, and received as payoff a sense of inclusion that I pocketed as greedily as any bought jockey does the profits of his corruption.

Sometimes things got contentious between us. Nancy would ask me to help her load the dishwasher and then chastise me for not adequately rinsing the plates beforehand. "How many times do I have to tell you, Denny? If you don't get every little bit of food off, what's left will end up caked on. Look at what you missed."

I made a remark to the effect that if you ended up having to wash the dishes by hand, what was the point of owning a dishwasher in the first place? This did not go over well.

"At this rate, I shudder to think what kind of household *you'll* keep," Nancy said, "that is, assuming you ever get married."

On another occasion à propos of nothing—she said, "Anne had such a lovely figure! Slender waist, graceful neck. You should lose a few pounds, Denny. Then you might get a boyfriend."

It was the same as with Daphne and her hair—or so I told myself, as I tried to swallow back my hurt. For that was my method of justifying Nancy's cruelty. If such abuse was simply part of how mothers treated daughters, then I should be grateful for it. This was what I had missed, and longed for. This was what it meant to be a daughter.

Still, I cannot deny that in my own subtle way, I gave as good as I got. Ernest was the linchpin in this. One Saturday in

February, when Nancy had had to run out to deliver Ben to a make-up flügelhorn lesson, he cornered me a second time, near the percolator.

"Such a plump little thing," he muttered in my ear. "With all that filthy stuff you type for me, you must have dirty dreams. Won't you tell me your dirty dreams?"

Of course, I could have pushed him away. It would have been the simplest thing in the world to push him away. But I didn't. Instead I turned, placed my lips against his ear, and whispered, "I dream about you."

Three

O NE OF MY duties as Ernest's secretary was to edit—in fact, to rewrite—his articles and grant applications under the guise of "typing" them. He would hand me a wad of illiterate notes, and I would transform it into a coherent piece of prose, which I would hand back to him. Then he would praise my "typing" skills. At first his ineptitude as a writer shocked me—I'd always taken it for granted that to get as far as he had in academia, you'd at least have to be able to craft a decent sentence—but then I asked myself why the gift for generating ideas should necessarily go hand in hand with the capacity to express them. If I had a greater facility with English than Ernest did, it was simply further proof that my own talents were of a purely clerical—and therefore limited— sort. Only later did I come to question this assumption, to look back at those books of Ernest's that I'd edited—no, *written*— and recognize the degree to which my improvements and refinements had really changed his ideas, making them as much mine as his. At the time, though, it would never have occurred to me to ask for any kind of credit. I was a secretary. "Typing" was my job.

One Saturday, after Nancy and I had finished playing, Ernest asked me to come up to his office above the garage to look over a manuscript with him. Nancy didn't object; I suppose she thought me too fat and unattractive to take seriously as a rival. Off she went to the supermarket (a Saturday ritual for her). Ernest led me out of the kitchen and into the garage and up the narrow staircase to the converted attic where he saw his patients. This was a cramped little space under the eaves, with ceilings and walls that bled into each other, so that you could hardly say where one began and the other ended. There was an Eames Case Study daybed upholstered in nubbly red fabric—presumably it was upon this that Ernest's patients lay while he probed their childhoods—and over it a picture of Freud, and over the desk, which faced the one window, a few model airplanes on strings. Ernest sat at the desk, and I sat on the daybed. Already we had a certain routine down for this sort of work: He would give me a manuscript, and I would read it aloud. (This one concerned Patient X, who refused ever to drink water; she even brushed her teeth with Coca-Cola.) Then I would read, and as I did, he would periodically interrupt me to amplify some thought, or grope toward a clarification—my cue to suggest, ever so delicately, a means of making his point more cleanly. Nor was it only a matter of writing; sometimes I would be emboldened to call attention to some half-baked supposition, or to propose a more persuasive interpretation. And yet between his natural ego and my natural diffidence, we were able to pretend that all I was doing was taking a complicated form of dictation. Whether privately he recognized the true extent of my contribution I'm still not sure.

After we had finished, Ernest stood up from his chair and sat next to me on the daybed. I said not a word. At this point it had been almost a month since the grope in the kitchen; if anything, I wondered why he had waited so long to make another move. I tried to make it clear, from my expression, that I was ready and willing, but he seemed reluctant to touch me, and finally, out of impatience, I put my hand on the back of his head and pulled his mouth toward mine. Everything happened very quickly then; his lovemaking, on this occasion as it would be on others, seemed to be a kind of payback for the help I had just given him—payback in the sense of vengeance as well as reward, for mixed into his passion were distinct tones of both gratitude and punishment. I didn't mind. I'd never had much of an appetite for namby-pamby sex. Then we sat together, half undressed, and he talked a little: about how irritating he found Ben's food phobias, and about Daphne's lack of respect for her parents, and about what he called, using the parlance of the day, Nancy's "frigidity." This last accusation, I would later learn, is one to which husbands often resort when they feel the need to justify, after the fact, an extramarital dalliance. At the time, though, it was totally new to me. I took it at face value, and felt as sorry for Ernest, whose needs Nancy obviously refused to satisfy, as I did for Nancy, condemned by her own coldness to miss out forever on the wild pleasures of sex.

I was always rather fond of Ernest's office above the garage. I liked the way the nubbly red fabric felt against my back, just as I liked the portrait of Freud, gazing down on us like some benevolent saint, and the smell of typewriter ribbons and wood and paper. Indeed, we might have gone on for years like that, our affair confined to those Saturdays and that daybed, had not Nancy decided rather capriciously one Saturday to forego her weekly trip to the supermarket and make lunch instead. Perhaps she suspected something, or perhaps she was starting to feel left out, or perhaps (this seems most likely) her decision had nothing to do with us, and was made in response to some shift in her own cosmos of which we knew nothing. In any case, after that Ernest stopped asking me up to his office, and we took to meeting at my apartment, usually on Sundays. In this way Nancy contributed, albeit unknowingly, to the intensification of our affair.

I suppose at this point I am obliged to offer some detailed explanation of what I felt about my situation at that time, as for most readers the ease with which I alternated between such seemingly incompatible functions—efficient secretary, available mistress, best friend to wife—must seem peculiar. For me, though, it was not peculiar at all. It was natural. Call me immoral, but as I typed out Ernest's correspondence outside his office each weekday, I felt no need to block from my memory the afternoons we spent making love. Nor when we made love did I feel stabs of guilt in recalling the mornings I played piano with Nancy. I moved easily among these roles. Of course I recognized the risks—among them the certainty that if Nancy ever found out about Ernest and me, I would be banished forever from Florizona Avenue, and have to quit my job—and yet I attributed those risks entirely to the narrowness of other people, and figured that so long as Ernest and I played our cards right, and no one found us out, there would be nothing to worry about. After all, he had as little wish for Nancy to discover our affair as I did. He was not one of those men who uses his mistresses to get back at his wife. He didn't want to leave her for me, and I didn't want to marry him. I adored them both. And so we proceeded fairly harmoniously, although I would be dishonest if I did not admit to sometimes experiencing a sense of emptiness in the aftermath of his departures, something akin to what one feels when one arrives home alone after a Thanksgiving dinner. For there *was* one thing that I would have liked (not that I ever could have had it), and that was to have a bed of my own at that house, if not Daphne's then some other bed, specifically designated for me. Not a bed I would sleep in every night, and certainly not Nancy's half of the huge bed with the slub linen spread: I still treasured my independence. Yet was it too much to hope that someday my role within the family might be legitimized?

Marriage remains, for me, a mysterious institution. For instance, Ernest and Nancy often argued in my presence. If our practice session was going late, and he needed my help with a chapter from his book, he would feel no compunction about striding into the living room and shouting, "When the hell are you two going to be done?" To which Nancy—not missing a measure—would reply, "Hold your horses," and continue playing. Ernest would storm out again, only to reappear a few minutes later to repeat his demand. She yelled, he left, he returned. With almost blithe disinterest they threatened and rebuffed each other, their voices rising, the level of tension escalating—and then we would finish, and it would be as if nothing had happened. Nancy would announce gaily that she was going to Safeway; Ernest and I would head up to his office. "Like water off a duck's back," as my mother used to say, which made me wonder if this was the secret of marriage: to develop—no, not a thick skin; rather, a down at once fragile and light, by means of which you could shake off, in an instant, any unpleasantness and go about your business. Yet it would protect you, too. Marriage protected. I wished I could have known that feeling of safety, a safety so deep it meant you could say anything, and never have to calculate all that you stood to lose.

Just before Thanksgiving of 1968, Nancy received a letter from Anne Armstrong in which her friend announced that she had left her husband, Clifford, and was living in a rented apartment with a novelist called Jonah Boyd—recently hired as writer-in-residence at Bradford. Nancy took the news hard, and would not say why. Perhaps the casual ease with which Anne had abandoned her marriage made her wonder if staying with Ernest all these years had been a mistake; or perhaps the discovery that Anne was having an affair ignited some fear in her that Ernest might be doing the same thing. All I know for certain is that the Saturday Nancy got the letter, for the first and only time in all the years I knew her, she could not play. Her fingers shook so badly she could barely form them into a chord. At last, pleading a headache, she asked if I'd mind forgoing our weekly session this one time.

The full story came out over the course of the next several Saturdays—details, background, and Nancy's mess of a reaction, as Anne kept her abreast of developments through letters and phone calls, and Nancy passed the news on to me. She had no one else in whom she could confide. That Anne's life, since the Wrights' departure from Bradford, had taken such an eccentric if not downright self-destructive turn was something for which, it appeared, Nancy blamed herself. Perhaps if she had stayed, Nancy speculated, and thus not deprived Anne of the outlet that their piano playing provided, Anne never would have left Clifford in the first place. For without her, Anne had nothing in Bradford. No children. No friends. Only Clifford, a well-meaning if remote mathematician.

I learned more about Anne. She was younger than Nancy by five years. Because she came from Brooklyn, she often expressed a longing for concerts and restaurants and galleries—all categories of experience in which Bradford, especially in the sixties, was sadly lacking. All Bradford had was a coffin factory. Anne never fit in easily with the other faculty wives, their malign chitchat, the bridge afternoons over which a cigarette haze hung, as well as a faint stink of gin. Clinking noises: ice against glass, glass against tabletop, engagement ring against wedding ring on fingers the nails of which were lacquered the color of plums. On these occasions, Anne sometimes drank. Too much. She never managed to pick up the finer points of bridge. She was tranquil only with Nancy, who somehow kept her recklessness in check. On her own, without Nancy to supervise, Anne became obstreperous. She had her ears pierced, and started introducing the word "orgasm" into bridge table conversation. (Usually the context was Clifford's failure to give her any.) Not that there was anything wrong with Clifford to look at, Nancy said. He was big and hirsute and possessed of a sort of blond, bland handsomeness that Nancy, at least, appreciated. And yet the very qualities that had attracted Anne to him when they had married—his even temper, his tactfulness, the reluctance ever to raise his voice that had seemed so refreshing to her, after her loud Brooklyn childhood—began, soon enough, to bore and then to vex her. She had a need for stimulation that Clifford could not fathom. "Entertain me! Amuse me!" she would beg when he came home from school, and he would tell her about the Fibonacci numbers, a sequence in which each entry is the sum of the two that precede it (1, 1, 2, 3, 5, 8, 13, 21 . . .) "The Fibonacci numbers," he would say, "are often repeated in the floral patterns and leaf arrangements of plants." Then he would show her a fir cone, ask her to examine its spirals. "As if I was one of his goddamn students," she complained to Nancy, who tried to placate her, telling her that she should be more patient. Clifford meant well. He was trying. But Anne would have none of it. "I keep expecting him to say, 'There'll be a quiz on this afterward,'" she said. "I tell you, I cannot bear it anymore. I cannot bear it."

Anne and Nancy had this conversation in 1966. Later that year, the Wrights moved west. It was then that things really fell apart. Deprived of Nancy's cautionary influence, Anne started going braless in public. She took to wearing hoop earrings, satin blouses in hot colors, and wraparound, tie-dyed skirts. Also sandals. She was a protohippie faculty wife at a time when not even the most rebellious female undergraduate would have dared anything more bohemian than tights. Nor did Anne cut a bad figure, according to Nancy, for she had a sort of gypsy prettiness that these outfits accentuated. Her hair fell in waves over her breasts, which were high and ample. To make it more red, she washed it with henna. To make her eyes darker and rounder, she smeared the lids with kohl. She was a graceful dancer, when she got the chance, with agile feet. (Also hands—hence her talent for the piano.) Yet she rarely got the chance. Clifford, "with his big clodhoppers," got in the way. He was like a bear, and when he danced— which was rarely—it was with the grim, embarrassed dedication of a dancing bear.

In September 1968, Anne went to a party in Bradford, a regular event hosted by the provost to welcome the year's crop of new faculty. Clifford, who had a cold, stayed home. Here she was introduced to Jonah Boyd. At this point, Boyd was in his late forties; he had just published his second novel, and it had gone down, in his own words (which Anne quoted), "like a lead balloon." But then a friend had gotten him a gig teaching creative writing to undergraduates at Bradford—"as if such a thing could be taught," Anne quoted him as saying. "*Creative writing*. What would Byron have made of such a term? What would Pope have made of it? Mockery. All 'creative writing' means is a chance for the brats to indulge themselves."

Anne was fascinated. She had never met a writer before, and told him so. He got her a drink. He himself did not drink, he explained, because he was a drunk. "Huh?" Anne said. This was back in the days when social drinking, far from being frowned upon, was the principal leisure activity of the academic classes, and most people who worked at universities drank like fish. Regenerate alcoholics had not yet become the staple of television talk shows that they are today, and former inebriates who had gone off the sauce were usually as reticent in their newfound sobriety as in the past they had been secretive in their intoxications. Yet Boyd not only admitted that until recently he had been, in his own words, a "boozer," he seemed to take an almost gustatory satisfaction in describing the depths of wretchedness to which "the bottle" had dragged him. For it was his intention, he said, to write a great novel, and contrary to all the nonsense spouted about Hemingway, you could not write a great novel if you were a drunk. Great writing required an evenness of disposition that the fuzzing haze of alcohol obliterated. Anne listened raptly, and drank. Curiously, he seemed to have no problem with *her* drinking. He kept fetching her fresh gin and tonics. He was a handsome man, if oddly foppish, with his bow tie and manicured mustache. In certain ways he reminded her of Clifford—who better embodied "evenness of disposition" than Clifford?—and yet in other ways he was so much less restrained, so much easier to talk to, that she found herself wondering what had induced her to marry Clifford in the first place.

They retreated to a sofa. People were watching them— colleagues, wives of colleagues, women whose husbands might tell Clifford what they had seen. She didn't care. Boyd's openness—his obliviousness to convention—had brought her past caring. Such openness, she knew, might have nothing to do with her. It might be a side effect of his having been a drunk, or of his being a novelist. Yet how much more pleasant if it turned out that she herself had inspired this response from him, this intuitive trust that allowed him to speak to her of things about which, with others, he would have stayed silent! If that were the case, then Anne owed it to him to be equally forthcoming.

She touched his collar. Lightly, just for a fraction of a second. Still, the gesture was noticed. She could feel a prickle of unease leap about the room. They were being watched, which both amused and emboldened her. Was he married? she asked. Sort of, he answered. Sort of? Well, he was in the middle of a divorce. This too, in Anne's sphere, was a novelty, and she asked for details. He and his wife, Boyd said, had been married straight out of high school. They had three children. For nineteen years they had lived together in a ranch house outside of Dallas, where his wife worked for the company that published the yellow pages, and Boyd cobbled together a living out of odd teaching jobs, while devoting the principal part of his energies to drinking and writing, in that order. The house was never clean, nor were the kids. "Cat scratches on the sofa, holes in the children's socks. It wasn't that we were poor. Oh, we *were* poor—just not to that degree. We could have afforded to buy our son a new pair of socks. The problem was, we couldn't get our act together. We were drunk all the time."

"How awful."

"It gets worse," he said. "I beat her."

Anne's eyes widened.

"I mean, badly. I put her in the hospital twice. Broke her collarbone. The second time I felt justified, because I'd caught her with someone else."

Now this was exciting. Had they been having this conversation thirty years later, Anne might have walked away, frightened or disgusted. According to the standards of Bradford in 1968, though, physical violence was forgivable in men, a natural response to having their virility stifled or thwarted, to the provocations of a shrewish wife. *She pushed me over the edge, the bitch.* Boyd had not said these words, yet if he had, Anne's reaction—arousal, combined with surprise that Boyd, now so pinkly sincere, could have ever been capable of taking such decisive action—would only have been enhanced.

It can sometimes take very little to propel one into a fatal decision, especially when there is nothing—not children, not patience, not a sense of duty—to hold one back. Anne left Clifford the next day, and moved in with Boyd. Until their divorces came through, they shared a cheap one-bedroom apartment, in a complex with cinder-block walls near a highway overpass. Her decampment titillated the faculty wives, and worried Nancy, who seemed uncertain whether her reaction ought to be one of maternal disapproval or sisterly support. In the end, she split the difference—the wrong thing

41

to do, as it turned out—and wrote a letter in which she both warned Anne that she ought to "think twice" and wished her well. Offended (yet she refused to explain why), Anne stopped calling. The flow of letters dwindled to a trickle. This was the thing that hurt Nancy the most. She was not invited to the wedding, which took place in January—an omission not to be taken personally, Anne assured her in a rare, rather cool letter, as in fact *no one* had been invited to the wedding: not Jonah's children, nor Anne's parents, nor any of his colleagues; only another novelist and her husband, new friends, who would act as witnesses. By way of a present, Nancy sent an expensive crystal bowl that in its very lavishness was meant to carry a message of injury and rebuke. By way of reply, she received a cursory thank-you note on lilac-scented paper. And then, for almost a year, Bradford went silent.

Four

L ATE ONE CLOUDY afternoon in the middle of July, the members of the Wright family, along with a small contingent of friends and neighbors, gathered in the driveway of 302 Florizona Avenue to bid Mark Wright goodbye. Earlier that week, watching the draft lottery on the little television in the kitchen with his mother, Mark had learned that his draft number was four. In the intervening days, all sorts of desperate measures had been proposed and dismissed. Orville Boxer suggested that Ernest ask one of his psychiatrist friends to write a letter asserting that Mark was a homosexual, but Ernest wouldn't hear of it. Then Ken Longabaugh advised that Mark bite the bullet and enlist, since with his education he'd most likely be given an intelligence post anyway, as Ernest had been during World War II; yet this proposition Mark himself wouldn't hear of, not because he objected to war per se (otherwise he would have declared himself a conscientious objector) but because in recent weeks he had undergone a crash course in radical politics, and now he understood that the war in Vietnam was merely part of a corrupt imperialistic campaign spearheaded by Henry Kissinger to suppress the will of the Vietnamese people; he would fight gladly, he said, if he could fight on the side of the North Vietnamese. At this Ernest

43

threw up his hands, and Nancy wept, but there was to be no more arguing. And so that July afternoon, along with two friends from Wellspring, both of them hippies with stringy hair and none-too-clean faces, Mark loaded into a battered Datsun with no reverse gear, his eventual destination the Canadian border, and a future the repercussions of which we could only guess at.

That morning Nancy loaned me her camera and asked me to take some pictures of the assembled, one of which I still have. In it the Wrights and their friends are posed clumsily in the driveway, in front of that famous Datsun that would later play as crucial a role in the family lore as the black Ford Falcon with red interior. In the front, Mark kneels between his scruffy friends. His expression is grave, and there is just a whisper of a beard on his chin. Behind him stands Daphne, holding a tin containing some chocolate chip cookies she had baked that morning as a farewell present, and next to Daphne stands Mark's girlfriend, Sheila, her hair tied in a single braid that drapes over her shoulder and hangs below her belt, and next to Sheila, the bizarre Boxers, both victims of the McCarthy blacklist, and hence eager to show their support of Mark in this gesture of defiance. Nancy is slightly to Bertha Boxer's right, her arms crossed tightly over her chest, while to *her* right, Hettie Longabaugh, who always managed to be around at dramatic moments, perches on one foot and casts a solicitous and possibly lewd glance at Ernest, who is hunched at a little distance from the others. From his expression you can see that this theatrical and overly public departure his wife has orchestrated embarrasses him deeply, that given his druthers, he would prefer for Mark to leave furtively, under cover of darkness. But there is nothing to be done about that.

The only person missing from the picture is Ben, and that is because, just at the moment that I was about to snap it, he separated himself from his parents and ran off toward the garage, against which he put his face. Today I can still feel his presence to the right of the yellowing frame, as remote from the rest of the family as Pluto from the other planets, and with an orbit just as eccentric.

Oh, what a sad and peculiar ceremony that was! None of us had any clue as to how we should behave. We were like wedding guests at that moment just after the reception when the bride and groom climb into a car dragging tin cans and drive off into some glorious future, leaving us to clean up the rice we have just thrown—only that day there was no rice, there were no tin cans, and the future into which these boys were driving, far from glorious, was possibly tragic. Eyes stern, Mark bade his farewells to the assembled, hugged his mother, kissed his girlfriend, shook his father's hand. His brother's hand he tried to shake too, but Ben refused to look at him, so Mark simply patted him on the shoulder, provoking a visible shudder. And then he climbed into the passenger seat of the Datsun, and the dirtier of his two friends, who was driving, started up the engine, and because the car had no reverse gear, he had to circle over the lawn, damaging the border grass, which made Ernest wince. "Goodbye!" Daphne called as the Datsun veered out of the driveway, and then at that instant she realized that she had forgotten to give Mark the cookies. "Wait, wait!" she cried, running after the car, which had turned the curve, and was out of view. Daphne burst into tears, and Nancy said, "Now what good is crying going to do anyone?" and stomped into the house, leaving the rest of us to stare at the space where moments before Mark had stood, and who knew if he would ever again stand there? Dusk was falling. We all trooped inside after Nancy for coffee and the forgotten cookies—everyone except Ben, who had retreated to the barbecue pit, where he remained until well after dark with a flashlight, writing a poem.

Some years later, Ernest told me that in his professional opinion Ben was doomed from the start, because insofar as Nancy was concerned, he could never hope to live up to his brother. And it is true that from the July day Mark drove off to Canada, his handsome face, by virtue of its enforced removal, suddenly seemed to be everywhere in that house. From the kitchen countertop next to the television, and Nancy's bedside table, and the mantel in the dining room, versions of Mark smiled out at us, a constant reminder that he was not where he should have been. Mark had always been an easier child than either of his siblings: wholesomely athletic, even-tempered, a favorite of all his teachers. At Wellspring he had majored in political science, and would have graduated cum laude had the disaster of the draft lottery not interrupted his otherwise effortless ascent. But it had, and now he was living in the most tenuous of exiles, a fugitive who would be jailed if he even dared to come back to his mother's house for Thanksgiving. As if to craft for himself an identity more in keeping with his new outlaw status, he grew his hair long; sent back snapshots of himself, scrawny and bearded, that made Nancy weep with pride. "He looks almost holy," she'd tell me. "Like Saint Francis, or Saint Blaise." For Nancy, draft dodging amounted to a kind of martyrdom.

Today, when the saga of the draft dodgers is talked about at all, it is usually as a sort of sidebar to the greater drama that was Vietnam itself. In 1969, though, the fate of these young men troubled the American conscience at least as much as that of the soldiers who were starting to return from the war maimed or dead or with pregnant Vietnamese wives in tow. And nowhere was this more the case than on Florizona Avenue: After all, of the twenty-four houses on that street, three had sent sons to Canada, whereas none had sent sons to Vietnam. Their affluence protected Nancy and her neighbors, allowing them the luxury of worrying about children who were safe and well-fed in row houses in Vancouver or Toronto instead of bleeding on the fields of battle. At least this was how I saw it. I never dared voice this opinion to Nancy, who would have considered it treasonous, and thrown me out of the house.

Ernest, by contrast, understood, and to some degree shared, my skepticism. Although he distrusted Richard Nixon, and loathed Kissinger, he had also inherited from his immigrant father a patriotic belief in America as a land of possibility whose principles it was a citizen's duty to defend, and therefore he could do no more than tolerate Mark's flight to Canada. At heart he was a deeply conformist man, his Freudianism of an old-fashioned and narrow variety that inclined him to regard all types of atypical behavior as pathologies for which it was the physician's duty to seek a therapy. And what was more nonconformist than a son who had not only broken with his country but broken the law? Or a wife who stormed out of dinner parties whenever the host happened to say something with which she was in political disagreement? For in the wake of Mark's departure, Nancy had taken up the mantle of his radicalism, and now, rather than hosting faculty wives teas, she organized petition drives for a variety of antiwar groups. Ernest would come home to find mobs of hippies parked in the living room, eating brownies and discussing protest strategies. Her outspokenness offended both his natural tactfulness and his abhorrence of what he called "scenes"—and now she was making them all the time. For instance, one afternoon at the faculty club, Bess Dalrymple, the elderly and soft-spoken wife of the retiring history chair, made the mistake of blithely quoting her husband's opinion that the draft dodgers "were no better than deserters and deserved to be shot." Nancy, eavesdropping at the next table, leapt up and let the poor thing "have it with both barrels," as she put it—barraging Mrs. Dalrymple with rhetoric until the foggy old creature burst into weeping and had to take refuge in the ladies' room. For Ernest this was the last straw, and not only because from that day on Jim Dalrymple—chivalrous to the last—stopped speaking to him; also because the episode confirmed that Nancy was no longer in any way under his control. "Let her send Mark money," he told me later. "Let her write letters to congressmen, letters to senators. But for God's sake, let her shut up."

In retrospect, I often wonder what it must have been like for Ben, those months after his brother's departure, watching his parents' marriage degenerate into a rancorous silence. At least Daphne had her burgeoning love affair with Glenn to retreat into; Ernest had me; Nancy had her various subcommittees and commissions and meetings. But Ben, in a way that at the time, I think, none of us understood or acknowledged, was alone. He had no friends to speak of, most of his coevals on Florizona Avenue having long since dismissed him as a loser or freak. I myself avoided, as much as possible, meeting his eye. That testy encounter at the hairdresser's had set the tone for our acquaintanceship, which would for years after be marked by unease on my part and on his by a remoteness bordering on hostility. Perhaps he never forgot the clinch in which he had caught his father and me that first Thanksgiving. Perhaps he simply didn't like me. Nor can I pretend, at this stage, that I much liked him.

As I saw it, Ben at fifteen had only one salient characteristic, and that was brattiness. It never occurred to me to wonder what might lie behind his more bizarre behavior (for example, his food phobias), for I was young myself then, and heedless of any suffering I could not exploit. Instead I wrote him off as simply a source of interruption. It seemed that he lived to pester, to complain to his mother about her cooking, or interrupt our four-hand to demand that she listen to one of his poems. He was always writing poems. He never did his homework, and his grades suffered accordingly. And Nancy, I am sorry to say, rather than informing him in crisp tones that there was a moment to read poetry and that this was not it, usually buckled under to his insistence, stopping whatever she was doing to listen to him and then responding to his recitations with that brand of offhand, reckless praise that in most cases speaks more to a parent's desire to get a kid off her back than to any genuine enthusiasm or belief in his talent. She had learned the hard way that offering criticism was a mistake, since with Ben even the mildest complaint invariably provoked a wail of frustration, an enraged "You just don't understand!" after which he would run off to his room, slamming the door behind him. Much easier to provide the balm of immoderate laudation. Still, I sometimes wondered if she went too far. For instance: "Mark my words," she told him once, "you'll be the youngest person to win the Nobel prize for poetry." A fateful exhortation, as it turned out, for he did mark her words—he forgot nothing—and later, when the youthful success she had forecast failed to materialize, he blamed her.

As a poet, Ben was both ambitious and lazy. He never revised, appeared oblivious to basic principles of spelling and grammar, took little care to type up clean copies or to follow the rules of poetic form. Thus his sonnets never scanned, while his villanelles were approximate at best. Generally speaking I thought his poems tendentious and humorless, though I never told Nancy this. Even so, starting when he was about twelve (and with her blessing) he began sending them out by the dozen, and not only to contests and publications specifically aimed at teenagers; also to such august publications as *Poetry* and *The New Yorker,* which invariably returned them with form rejection slips paper-clipped to each bundle. Then Nancy would rail at what she called the editors' "lack of vision." "It's a matter of who you know," she'd tell Ben, "an inside job"— evading the tricky question of why, if it was an inside job, she had encouraged him to send the poems out in the first place.

It was Ernest's contention (which he shared only with me) that Ben suffered from an underdeveloped sense of reality. In Ernest's view, Ben's problem was that he lived half in a world of dreams, the borders of which he could not clearly delineate; much of his bad temper and frustration, his father felt, owed to the refusal of the "real world" (whatever that was) to conform to his wishes. A reasonable diagnosis, I thought at the time— and yet today I cannot help but wonder whether in this regard Ben differed all that much from most other writers. Everything that Ernest said of him, for example, he could just as easily have said of Jonah Boyd. Also, I think it would be a mistake to understate the degree to which Nancy encouraged Ben in his delusions, if for no other reason than because they lent ballast to her own: that she had been a perfect mother, and that her children, thanks to everything she had done for them, would go far. So she abandoned him. This is awful but true. The only person who might have gotten through to Ben at this time was Mark, and Mark was long gone, though Ben spoke eagerly of the Easter break when Nancy had promised that he could fly to Vancouver for a visit. (Mark didn't want his parents to come.) Ben was proud to have a rebel for a brother, and put Mark's picture above his bed, and made a FREE MARK WRIGHT button out of red and blue construction paper that he wore to school every day for a week, until one of his teachers infuriated him by pointing out the illogic of the message, given that Mark had gone to Canada of his own free will.

It was around this time that the so-called nosebleed incident occurred. One morning Nancy rose later than usual, went into Ben's room to make his bed, and found the sheets and walls spattered with blood. In a panic she threw a coat over her nightgown and rushed over to the high school, where she tracked Ben down in his gym class, one of two dozen boys waiting to throw a basketball at a hoop. And there she pounced on him, at once relieved that he was alive and furious that he had given her such a scare. It turned out that during the night he had had a nosebleed (he was prone to them), woken, sneezed blood all over the wall and bedclothes, and fallen back asleep. Then in the morning he had dressed in the dark and left without even realizing what had happened. And now here was his mother, a harridan in pink slippers and a raincoat, a scarf tied over her hair, hurling herself at him in front of a group of boys who would never forget what they had witnessed, or let him forget it.

Years later, when he was famous and people cared about his

life, he described the incident. In a memoir titled *The Eucalyptus,* he wrote: "My mother's intrusive arrival at the school that morning merely confirmed what I already suspected: that she was a meddler and an hysteric. At the same time, it opened my eyes to a certain ferocity in her character of which I had so far only caught glimpses. Later she told me that it was my brother as much as me of whom she was thinking, when she switched on the light in my bedroom and saw all that blood: Mark, his body bullet-riddled, or dismembered, in some remote theater of war. And so, as she put on her coat that morning, she made a vow to God that if I were to be spared, she would devote the rest of her life to the protection of her children. And I was spared. And yet it was a fatal pact, because by making it, she was effectively telling us that our safety mattered more to her than our loving her, or feeling that she loved us; that she would rather have us safe at a great remove than at danger near her.

"I now see that the reason I myself decided never to have children is because I knew I could never be as selfless as my mother."

Five

I T W A S A Saturday morning near the end of October 1969. I was sitting next to Nancy at the piano when the telephone rang. As was her habit, she jumped up to answer it, in case it was Mark, calling collect from Vancouver. But it was not Mark. It was Anne Boyd. I could tell, because after the initial "Hello," Nancy's voice rose into a girlish squeal that meant pleasure greater than anything I could induce. "Annie, Annie!" she cried—and pulled the phone, which had a long cord, into the study.

I got up from the piano. The realization that for the moment, at least, my services would not be needed filled me with a giddy sense of freedom, as if school had been canceled for the day. So I puttered around the living room, flicking dust off the nesting tables and repositioning the cushion that covered Dora's pee stain on the leather chair, all the while listening in on Nancy's half of the conversation. "Oh, but that's wonderful! What do you mean? Don't be ridiculous, of course you can stay with us. Now, Anne, I don't want to hear another word about it. You'll stay here and that's final. No, I don't even want to hear the word 'hotel' . . . Good. When will you get in? We'll pick you up at the airport. Okay, if you'd rather . . . But how will you know how to find the house? I'm hopeless with directions, you'd better have Clifford—I mean Jonah—call back when Ernest's here. Oh, Annie, I'm sorry about that. Will you ever forgive me? I'm just so used to your husband being Clifford! Tell Jonah I'm dying to meet him. We all are. Annie, I can't wait to see you, it's been so long . . . Yes, have him call tonight. Ernest should be back by seven. Right. We'll be waiting. Bye."

She hung up. "Denny, you'll never believe it," she said, sweeping back into the living room. "That was Anne Armstrong. I mean, Anne Boyd. I haven't head from her in a year. And now guess what? She and her husband—her new husband—are coming for Thanksgiving."

"Really? How wonderful."

"Yes, isn't it?" Nancy's hands flew to her face. "Oh, but there's so much to do! I mean, this man she's married—this Jonah Boyd—he's a published writer. We've got to put him up in the style to which he's accustomed."

I was tempted to ask why she thought that published writers would be accustomed to any particular kind of style, then thought better of it, and followed her into Daphne's room. It was the first time I'd ever been in there. With a queenly gesture, Nancy flung open the curtains, letting through a slant of late morning light that exposed the moss green carpeting, a double bed with a rumpled floral coverlet. Along one wall were bracketed bookshelves on one of which Ayn Rand's *Atlas Shrugged* elbowed an assortment of high school textbooks. On another was Daphne's collection of frog figurines. Two posters—a psychedelic peace sign and the cover of Bob Dylan's *Blonde on Blonde* album—had been thumbtacked to the wall. Below them lay a heap of stuffed animals and dirty clothes. "Oh, well, I suppose it will have to do," Nancy said, putting her hands on her hips and surveying the wreckage. "Of course, Daph will have to clear away all of her crap." She tossed a pink elephant onto the pile, then sat down on the bed. "Oh, but this mattress! Feel it!"

I sat down next to her. I felt.

"The springs are shot. And these sheets! I'll have to buy a new bed, that's all there is to it. And new bed linens. You know the reason they're coming—he's supposed to give a lecture up in San Francisco. Someone else was supposed to give it, some very famous poet, but the poet went into a drunk tank, and they asked the husband—Jonah Boyd—to take his place. Now why do you think she wants to visit? Does she miss me? I hope nothing's wrong. They'll fly into LAX Thanksgiving morning, drive over, stay two nights, and then on Saturday head up north, stopping for a few days at Big Sur on the way. And the best part is, Anne and I will have plenty of time to play. Finally we can take another crack at the Grand Duo."

I pretended both surprise and pleasure. It was obvious that Nancy needed a sounding board for her fretfulness and planning impulses; also an assistant in what was clearly going to be a redecoration project of considerable scope. And so that very afternoon, along with Daphne—whose outrage at being thrown out of her room Nancy had managed to quell, somewhat, by promising to let her to pick out the sheets—I was taken to Macy's, first to the furniture department, where Nancy arranged for immediate delivery of a new Serta Perfect Sleeper, and then to the whites department, where Daphne, after much debate, settled on a set of "Vera" sheets decorated with bright orange sunsets and blue rainbows in the style of Peter Max. Here the trouble began. Nancy didn't like the sheets. She worried that Boyd—a novelist, after all—would

55

mock them in one of his books, follow a description of their psychedelic gaudiness with some insulting witticism, something like, "I had to wear sunglasses to bed." For Nancy, in addition to biographies of crowned heads, was an avid consumer of novels in which adulterous men and women parried rude remarks over martinis, and though she had not yet read any of Jonah Boyd's novels, she took it for granted that they would fit into this category. "Really, honey, couldn't we get something more subdued?" she asked Daphne, who had inherited her mother's stubbornness, if not her taste.

"But you said *I* could choose!" Daphne said. "You promised. After all, these people are only going to sleep on them two nights. But I have to sleep on them practically the rest of my life!"

In the end, to avoid a public scene, Nancy gave in on the sheets. Bags in tow, we hastened back to Florizona Avenue, where we found Ernest and Glenn in the study, smoking cigars and listening to Mahler's Fifth Symphony on the Harmon-Kardon stereo. Glenn and Daphne greeted each other with the studied casualness of people who don't want anyone to guess they've recently been in bed together; I could tell, because that was just how Ernest and I greeted each other.

As no dinner invitation appeared to be in the offing, I said my good-byes and went home. Back then I still lived in a one-bedroom apartment on Orechusetts Drive. My complex—essentially a stucco rectangle with views of the 420 free-way—was called Eaton Manor. Nearby were Cavendish Hall, Hampton Estates, and Chatsworth Court. Most of my neighbors were fellow secretaries, some of whom were also having affairs with their bosses. On Sunday afternoons, Ford LTDs and Oldsmobile Cutlasses filled the parking lot, taking up the empty spaces between the Chevy Novas and Dodge Darts. At this point, my relationship with Ernest had not yet settled into the durable bond that would later prove so sustaining for us both; it was still an off-and-on thing, fretful and fitful. Some Sunday afternoons he would arrive unannounced at my door, pinion me to the wall or push me onto the bed, where we would make rough love. Afterward I would give him tea or Coca-Cola, and we'd look at the television until dusk fell, when he'd leave with as few words as he had come, and I'd move to the window, to watch his car pull out of the parking lot and imagine what, back on Florizona Avenue, Nancy was up to: feeding the cat, or baking a ham, or knitting. I admit that at those moments I envied Ernest, with Dame Carcas to have to hurry home to.

Much has changed in the field of psychoanalysis during the years since Ernest practiced it in the office above his garage. Freud is no longer totemic, and today, if a therapist were to say to his patient, "Well, it's obvious: Even though it was the husband you were having the affair with, the one you were in love with was the wife," the patient, though she might agree or disagree, would hardly be shocked. And yet at the time, such an idea wouldn't even have occurred to Ernest, not because he rejected lesbianism as a category, but because he had yet to conceive of a universe in which men didn't always stand at the very center. Thus he would never have guessed that as I had sat next to Nancy on Daphne's bed that afternoon, a longing had swept through me which I could hardly articulate but which I now recognize to have been something akin to desire. Of course, it never would have occurred to me to try to kiss Nancy, or even embrace her. Nor, I suspect, would she have tolerated such advances. Still, the feeling was there, mixed up

57

strangely with my daughterly adoration. This was what drove me back to that house every Saturday, despite the abuse I had to endure. Since then, of course, I have known my own fair share of amorous adventure, I have been loved by several good men (Ernest among them) and in at least one case experienced a love far deeper than anything I ever felt for Nancy. So why is it that today I keep dreaming about that afternoon on Daphne's bed? What is it that I wanted to happen? Why is her voice—of which I have only a memory—so sharp and distinct in my head, and why, when I wake up in the middle of the night, am I tormented by her particular and peculiar smell of cigarettes and cooking and the perfume she wore only on special occasions, such as Thanksgiving, with notes of cassia and anise and bearing a name that would forever after connote, for me, that remote and lacquered world of womanhood in which she and Anne had spent such easy days, and which I could never penetrate—*Après l'Ondée*?

The day before Thanksgiving Nancy called and asked if I could stop by after work to help her get the house ready for the Boyds. I readily agreed. The pleasure of holidays, it has often seemed to me, is mostly anticipatory, which is perhaps why, today, I recall those hours that I spent cleaning and cooking with Nancy, scrubbing the bathtub while she ironed the "Vera" sheets and made the bed, with a far greater fondness than I do the dinner itself. She was in a euphoria of planning. Already she had hounded Daphne into putting away everything that gave her room a sense of identity. Gone were the books, the frog figurines, the posters. Two drawers had been emptied and part of the closet cleared. Her mother's orders Daphne obeyed flatly and without protest, since they fed a resentment the cultivation of which, at this stage in her life, was one of her principal occupations. With the pitiless dispassion of adolescence, of the child who believes that *she* will never make the mistakes that dog her elders, Daphne observed her mother as she went about the onerous routine of constructing a fictive guest room, a stage set to last only two nights. Ben watched too, though with greater empathy: Although he would not be leaving home for two years, already he had begun composing a poem of farewell, in which the protagonist, from the vantage point of his Wellspring dorm room, regards with smug compassion the spectacle of his mother at the supermarket, buying his favorite treats and then bursting into tears upon the realization that he will no longer be home to eat them. I know this because, several weeks later, he read the poem aloud to us. "Isn't he gifted?" Nancy asked, her eyes on the music desk.

As the afternoon wore away, Nancy grew more nervous. What would Anne look like? she wondered. Would she have quit smoking, gained weight, lost weight? "I wonder why she decided to come," Nancy said at the piano. "I mean, why she *really* decided to come. What do you think, Denny?"

"To see you, of course."

"Is that it, though? Is that all?"

We retreated to the kitchen, where we washed vegetables and tore up bread for the stuffing. It was now becoming clear that as much as it excited her, the prospect of Anne's visit also filled Nancy with dread. She confided that every time the phone rang, part of her hoped that it would be Anne, calling to cancel—"because then, at the very least, I wouldn't have to deal with any of it. The awkwardness, and having to explain about Mark, and the new husband." What if the old connection no longer surged? What if, on reuniting, she and Anne felt nothing, or worse (*was* it worse?) felt *too* much—a tug of longing so intense it could engender only sorrow, given how rarely they were now able to see each other? In the first case, she would greet Anne's departure with relief, in the second with regret, in both with an inconsolable ache of loss.

She did not sleep well that night (or so she told me the next morning). I came over early, and together we stuffed the turkey, taking care to adjust the thermometer before arranging it in its pan. Into the oven the bird went. Nancy took off her apron; lit a cigarette. She was harrowed by anxiety, while I, on the contrary, felt rising in me the richest flush of pleasure. That morning was the apogee of my love for Nancy, a love the name of which I dared not speak, and which I had tried, ironically, to consummate through my affair with her husband. Later I grew to love Ernest for himself; that Thanksgiving, he was an irrelevance. It was Nancy with whom I was besotted, and the passionate suitor, as all passionate suitors know, is profoundly selfish. How I longed for her to weep, just so that I could kiss away her tears! No matter that what preoccupied her was another love, no matter that I was as irrelevant to her, at that moment, as Ernest was to me! This was my chance to prove myself. So I bustled about, chopping carrots, setting the table, as effervescent as Daphne was sullen. I even took care, for once, to load the dishwasher to Nancy's exact specifications, and was disappointed when, rather than peering inside to make sure I'd misarranged the plates, she slammed the door shut and switched the thing on without a word—when for once I had done a perfect job!

It was close to one o'clock. Nancy was basting the turkey

for the umpteenth time. Dinner was scheduled for four, with the other guests invited for three. The Boyds' flight had landed, on time, at ten-thirty (Nancy had checked with TWA), which meant that they should have arrived in Wellspring at twelve-fifteen. Ernest was sequestered in his office above the garage. Ben and Daphne were playing Scrabble at the tulip table. Already Mark had made his mournful holiday call; tears had been shed at his description of Vancouver going about its regular business, an ordinary weekday in Canada, which he and some of his fellow draft dodgers were going to try to make more cheerful by preparing a little feast of their own, with a soy loaf in the shape of a turkey. The memory of that call must have touched some nerve of maternal affection in Nancy, for now she stole up behind Ben and rubbed his shoulders.

"Mom, stop," he said.

"*Lucid*," she whispered. "Right there, the double letter score—"

"Will you please not help him?" Daphne asked.

"Sorry. What time is it?"

"Five past one."

"I wonder why they haven't gotten here. Maybe they had an accident. Or got lost."

"Then they'd have called."

"Or maybe they pulled in for gas in a bad neighborhood and got held up," Ben interjected helpfully. "That happened to Hettie Longabaugh's sister, remember? People who don't know L.A.—"

"But if they rented a car, it would have a full tank."

"It's my fault," Nancy said. "I should have sent Ernest to pick them up."

Daphne switched on the television. "Poor mother, always so

worried," she said, with the easy gravity of a girl whom sex has endowed with delusions of maturity. "Anyway, a few hours in Compton would probably do them some good. Let them see how the other half lives, while we stuff ourselves with turkey."

"Maybe I should call the highway patrol—"

"Just give them another hour. They could have stopped for lunch."

"On Thanksgiving?"

Little Hans started to bark. "Oh, I hope that's them," Nancy said.

"It could be Glenn," Daphne said, adjusting her hair. "He said he might come early."

We all hurried to the front hall. Little Hans had his paws on the stained glass of the door, which Nancy opened. Outside a man and a woman in heavy East Coast coats were pulling luggage out of the trunk of a red Chevrolet.

"Anne, thank goodness!" Nancy cried, and ran to embrace her. They kissed and wept, and Anne introduced Jonah Boyd. Nancy reached for his hand; he pulled her closer and kissed her on both cheeks, which seemed both to fluster and please her. "Kids, come help with the luggage!" she yelled, and Daphne and Ben shuffled over to the car, pretending annoyance but obviously curious and not unhappy to see Anne again, and to meet her new husband. At first Anne held them at a distance, expressing astonishment at how much they had grown. Then, that convention dispensed with, she hugged them both.

Burdened with luggage, the group made its way into the house, Little Hans picking up the rear.

As for me, I hung back. No one had yet asked me to do anything.

I was introduced. Jonah Boyd appeared to be about forty-five. He had pink cheeks and a carefully groomed, salt-and-pepper mustache. His hair, given his age, was surprisingly luxuriant, his clothes immaculate—dark suit, white shirt, and striped tie. By contrast, Anne was wearing a wool coat that had been torn near the pocket and then clumsily restitched, and she carried an enormous, shapeless handbag. She had shaggy red hair that was graying at the roots, nicotine-stained teeth, a thick middle. Also, her eye makeup was smudged in a way that suggested she had been weeping.

All at once a sensation of misplaced triumph welled up in me. This Anne was a far cry from the willowy creature Nancy had described. Certainly they could never have shared clothes! I admit, my rival's sordid demeanor—not to mention the expression of concern and disappointment that claimed Nancy's face as she gave Anne the once-over—sparked in me an unexpected confidence, and I shook Anne's hand heartily. "I'm Denny, Dr. Wright's secretary," I said. "Welcome to California."

"So you're the new four-hand partner."

"Why yes," I answered with surprise. Until that moment, I'd had no idea that Nancy had even mentioned me to Anne.

"We all rely on Denny," Nancy said. Then she said, "Let me show you to your room," and led the Boyds down the hall. Daphne and I followed. "Ernest's in his office. He has a new office above the garage. He should be down in a few minutes."

"This is a wonderful house," Boyd said, in a rich, slightly cracked baritone.

"Oh, thanks. It's nothing fancy, but we like it. And here's the guest room."

Daphne winced.

We crossed the threshold into the newly made room, which indeed looked quite guest roomish. "Very nice," Boyd said.

"Wait a minute—" Anne stopped in her tracks. "I knew someone was missing. Where's Mark?"

"Oh, he's in Vancouver."

"Vancouver!"

"Yes. He went in July to assert his opposition to the war."

"You mean he's a draft dodger?"

Nancy's smile collapsed into a sort of tremble of the lips.

"Sweetheart, that's not a very nice way of putting it," Boyd said, resting a hand on his wife's shoulder in a gesture that might have been protective and might have been a warning. "Anyway, I, for one, stand completely behind the draft resisters. I fought in Korea, you know. A brutalizing experience. If I were in his shoes, I'd do the same thing."

"Thank you, Mr. Boyd."

"Jonah."

"Jonah. I appreciate that."

"Oh, Nancy, you must miss him," Anne said, sitting down on the bed. "And on Thanksgiving!"

Tears rimmed Nancy's eyes. "I do miss him," she said. "But I also respect that he's doing what he feels he has to." She straightened her back. "Well, you two must want to wash up. I've got the turkey to attend to. Whenever you're ready, just come into the living room, and Ernest will make everyone drinks."

We left, closing the door behind us. Back in the kitchen, Nancy blotted her eyes, gave Daphne an unwanted hug, and checked to see if the turkey's thermometer had popped. (It had not.) Then she arranged some crackers around a cheese ball rolled in pecans and a pile of rumaki, and we adjourned

64

to the living room, where Anne was settling herself on the cat-stained leather chair, Boyd on the sofa. By now it was fairly obvious, at least to me, that the Boyds had been fighting, and that this was probably why they had been late. You could tell from the puffiness of Anne's eyes, the slight rasp in her voice—a weeper's rasp, as opposed to a smoker's. And Boyd himself was smiling too broadly and talking too loudly, in that way of men who believe in always putting on a brave face, even when the house is falling down around them. Every now and then he shot a glance of irritation at his wife, who was clearly incapable of such emotion-masking niceties.

Soon Ernest came down from his eyrie. He kissed Anne, and shook Boyd's hand manfully.

"The Boyds would like drinks," Nancy said. In those days, women did not mix drinks.

"Certainly," Ernest said. "What'll it be?"

"Just Coca-Cola for me, thanks," said Boyd.

"And you, Anne?"

"Gin and tonic. And make it strong. After that trip, I need it."

"Oh, was there turbulence?" Nancy asked.

"Only in the car on the way from the airport."

Nancy gave a trill-like laugh. "Anne, always such a card!"

"No, but seriously, Ernest, I want your professional opinion on something."

"Honey, do we really have to go into all that?" Boyd asked.

"Be quiet, Jonah—it's about a problem that arose on the way here from the airport, and not for the first time, and frankly I'm very, very upset about this, even though my husband insists on pretending nothing's the matter."

"Oh yes?" Ernest said. (As a rule, psychoanalysts loathe being asked to give free advice.)

"Darling," Boyd said, "I really can't imagine why Dr. Wright should be remotely interested in our trivial little—"

"Ernest, you're a shrink. Wouldn't you agree that there's sometimes more to the trivial than meets the eye?"

"I suppose," Ernest said, handing Anne her drink, "though of course, as Freud himself noted, not everything has a hidden meaning. Sometimes a cigar and all that. Well, *cin-cin*."

"Cheers," said Nancy.

"This really is a beautiful house," Boyd said. "Why, do you know this is the first time in my life I've been to California?"

"He keeps losing them."

"Losing what?"

"Sweetheart—"

"His notebooks. That's why we were late. He left them on the plane, in the seatback pocket. We were halfway here in the car when suddenly he says, 'They're not in my briefcase.' And then we have to turn around and make a mad dash back to the airport and run screaming down the concourse to stop the plane before it takes off again."

"Notebooks?"

"Sorry, I should have explained. He writes in notebooks. His new novel."

"My lady wife is making a mountain out of a molehill," Boyd said. "It's true, in a moment of inattention, I left the notebooks in the seatback pocket, thinking I'd already put them in my briefcase. But then I realized they were missing, we went back to the airport, and I retrieved them. The cleaners had taken them off the plane and left them with the gate agent. All this running screaming down the runway—"

66

"The concourse."

"—running screaming down the concourse is my wife's somewhat hysterical embellishment."

Tears were suddenly streaming down Anne's cheeks. "You just don't understand," she said. "You don't realize how this is torturing me—"

"Excuse me," Ernest said, "but didn't you make a spare copy?"

"No, he did not! He refuses, simply refuses, no matter how much I beg him. See, Jonah? I'm not the only one who thinks this is craziness. Tell him it's craziness, Ernest."

"I'm not sure it's anything so grave as that," said Ernest, who was evidently becoming interested in spite of himself. "But I do think it would make sense—that it would be, well, practical—to keep a copy safe somewhere. As a precaution."

"Whenever we go on a trip, if Ernest's working on an article or something, he puts a copy in the refrigerator," Nancy said brightly, "because there, at least, it should be safe in case of a fire."

"I suppose it has always been my folly," Boyd said, "to trust to the protection of the muse."

Ernest raised his eyebrows, perhaps in response to Boyd's antiquated way of speaking, which could be charming or offputting, depending on your point of view.

"Do you see what I'm up against?" Anne asked. "I mean, here we are talking about this novel for which he's been paid a lot—I mean, a lot—of money, and that he claims to care about more than anything in the world, even more than me, he said once. And what does he do? He 'trusts to the protection of the muse.' Only the muse is falling down on the job! This spring, for instance—we were getting off the train in New York, when he dropped one of the notebooks between the platform and the train, right onto the tracks."

"Yes, and the stationmaster climbed down and got it for me, didn't he?"

"It must be terrifying to think you've lost something precious," Nancy said to no one in particular.

"Dropping something is not the same as . . . I mean, my wife makes it sound like a pattern, which it isn't. Just those two incidents, which, when you look at them closely, have nothing whatsoever to do with each other."

"Let's ask Ernest if they have anything to do with each other. Ernest?"

"I really couldn't say," Ernest said, scratching the back of his neck, "although I will repeat that I think it would probably be a smart idea to start making copies."

"And you know what?" Boyd said. "I agree." He held up his right hand. "How does this sound? I, Jonah Boyd, being of sound mind and body, vow that from this day forward I shall make copies of my notebooks thrice weekly." He put his hand down again. "There, does that make you feel better, darling?"

A quiet fell. Anne nursed her drink.

"Well, isn't it lovely to be with old friends for the holiday?" Nancy said.

"Yes indeed," I said.

"It is lovely to be in the hands of such a charming hostess, and to spend the holiday in such a charming house," Boyd said.

"Oh, Jonah!" Nancy said, blushing with pleasure and a susceptibility to Boyd's rather idiotic pleasantries that I must admit made me think less of her.

As for Anne, she was turning her glass round and round in

68

her hand, staring into the ice. Even from across the room I could see the smudge marks where she had pawed it.

A silence now ensued that was like the ash end of a cigarette—mesmerizing in its gradual attenuation, coming each second closer to collapse, until Nancy did the conversational equivalent of rushing in with an ashtray. "Well, I'm afraid that I, for one, need to be getting back to the kitchen," she said, and jumped up. "You'll excuse me, won't you?"

"I'll help," I said, rising to follow her.

"Me too," Anne said.

We all strode into the kitchen, where we found Glenn Turner sitting at the tulip table with Daphne and Ben. They were watching *Bonanza*. Nancy introduced Glenn to Anne. "At Thanksgiving, I always invite some of Ernest's grad students," she explained, "the ones who can't afford to fly home. I call them my 'strays.'"

"You look like a miniature version of Ernest in that bow tie," Anne said to Glenn, reeling a bit from her drink. "Oh, can I do the gravy? I love doing the gravy."

Nancy gazed at me—a little helplessly, if truth be told.

"Well, Denny, isn't that nice of Anne?" she said. "She's offered to do the gravy."

"Lovely," I said.

From inside the oven, a ping sounded. The turkey had popped.

Six

A NNE'S GRAVY WAS lumpy. I say this out of neither jealousy nor anger, but rather because I am determined to report these events truthfully, and not veer from the perspective of what I witnessed—what I knew at the time. Anne's gravy was lumpy, yet Nancy made a big fuss over it, saying that it was the best gravy she'd had in years, and asking what was her secret. All the while I sat in my usual place, two seats down from Nancy on the left, between Glenn and Phil Perry, who had arrived, as if by instinct, just as Ernest was cutting the first slice from the turkey breast. (Phil Perry was to me something of a nonentity in those years, which in retrospect I find frightening. That year the girl with the bangs was absent.)

I made no mention of it. I was very good. I even took a ladleful of the gravy myself, letting it dribble over my mashed potatoes, and pushing the little coagulated flour pellets to the side. Too much salt, too. All told, it was appalling gravy. It would have been a kindness if Nancy had said something to me to that effect, even just a few words in private, but she didn't.

At dinner, the conversation focused once again on Jonah Boyd's novel. It seemed that Ernest had filled Glenn in on what had happened, and now Glenn, too, was curious to learn more about these mysterious notebooks that Boyd had earlier mislaid—although, as Boyd now informed us, "notebook" wasn't really the right term. "The Italian word is *quaderna*," he explained. "They're actually blank books, of the most fantastic quality, bound in leather. I'll show you." And he leapt out of his chair, returning a few seconds later with an exemplar, which he passed around. "I first found these maybe six years ago, in Verona. It was my Guggenheim year, and I was on my way back to France from Venice, when I happened upon this amazing little shop in the medieval quarter. Leather and paper goods. The owner was a very aristocratic lady, very beautiful and ancient, and wearing a pair of snow-white gloves. She showed these to me, and I really thought they were the most beautiful things I'd ever seen. Works of art in themselves. So I bought up the stock—there were half a dozen—and ever since then I've had a standing order. Now I find I can't write in anything else."

"Excuse me," Glenn said, "but do you mean that literally—that you can't write in anything else—or that you *prefer* not to?"

"To tell the truth, I'm not absolutely sure. So far, thank heavens, I haven't found myself in a situation where I've had to do without."

"But what if the stock ran out? Or the notebooks stopped being manufactured?" Ernest asked.

"I pray that shall never happen. But if it does, I suppose I shall have to make do with plain old legal pads, as in the old days."

"It's worse than he says," Anne said. "Now he can only write with one pen. This very particular, very expensive

Waterman fountain pen. He's lost that, too, and had to replace it."

"Aren't the ways of writers fascinating?" asked Glenn, and handed me the notebook, which I inspected. The paper was gold-edged; the soft, cappuccino-colored leather gave off a scent of cloves. I passed it to Phil, who passed it to Ben, who opened it.

"Ben!" Nancy said. "Shut that at once! Mr. Boyd didn't give you permission to read his novel."

"Oh, but I don't mind," Boyd said. "He's welcome to read it. I love to share work-in-progress. Actually, I was thinking that if you were all amenable, perhaps after dinner I could read some of it aloud."

"Well, that would be wonderful," Nancy said—her voice a little hesitant, though, as if she were debating the social suitability of the proposition. "Only please don't feel that you have to."

"So long as you speak up if you get bored. It's important for writers to know when they've ceased to provide pleasure to an audience."

"What is your novel about?" asked Daphne.

"A good question, young lady, though difficult to answer. I suppose," he said after a moment, "that it's about the conflict between the Apollonian desire to touch the sun and the forces that seek to suppress it, to push us earthwards—"

"It's about balloons," said Ben, who was reading.

Anne laughed. I craned to get a look at the pages in the notebook: creamy in tone, the blue prose unfurling like ribbon, with hardly a blot or crossing out to be seen.

"Now Ben, you've held onto that for long enough. Pass it to your sister," Nancy said. "Besides, it's rude to read at the dinner table."

"He's right, though, it *is* about balloons," Anne said in a slur. "About a balloon crash, actually, that happened outside of Paris in the late nineteenth century."

"How fascinating." (Was Nancy relieved to learn that there was no way her sheets might enter into such a novel?) "I can promise you, Mr. Boyd—Jonah—we'll be the first to buy it. I'm an avid reader myself—mostly biographies. I love history. And Ben, my youngest, is a poet. He's very talented. He won a prize last year."

"A poet!" said Boyd. "How wonderful."

"Can I read one of my poems?" Ben asked.

"Oh, now, Ben," Nancy said, laughing.

"What's so funny? If he gets to read part of his book, I don't see why I shouldn't get to read one of my poems."

"But Mr. Boyd is a professional writer. I'm sorry," Nancy added to Boyd. "Sometimes Ben can be a little—"

"It's no skin off my back," Boyd said mildly. "If he wants to read, let him."

"Yes, why not?" Anne agreed. "After all, youth should have its say."

Ben—who had just handed the notebook, somewhat reluctantly, to his sister—looked imploringly at Nancy, who looked at Ernest, who was looking, rather unhelpfully, at the kitchen door.

Only later would I realize what a difficult moment this was for Nancy. The dilemma was this: Should she allow her child to read aloud his adolescent and sometimes asinine poetry, if by doing so he might bring embarrassment, even opprobrium, upon her? On the one hand, she didn't want to discourage him. On the other—and despite her newfound penchant for making scenes at the faculty club—she was at heart a woman who believed in subscribing to the public forms; otherwise invisible arbiters might make derogatory notations in immense volumes from which nothing could be erased. And just as earlier she had feared Jonah Boyd mocking her sheets, now she must have envisioned him incorporating into one of his novels some humiliating sequence in which a boy read bad poetry while his lamebrain mother smiled on.

It was all too much for her, and she answered, I am sorry to say, with a muddle. "Oh, Mr. Boyd—Jonah—that's so kind of you," she said. "But Ben's poetry . . . well, of course his father and I think it's very good . . . Still, I'm sure he wouldn't want to impose—"

"Yes I would," Ben said.

Anne laughed, sputtering a little wine.

"I assure you, Nancy, it would be no imposition at all," Boyd said. "Poetry comes as such a relief when you're mired in prose. Besides, there can be something so—refreshing—about a young voice."

Nancy looked doubtfully toward Ernest. "Well?"

"I don't see what harm it would do."

She smiled tightly. "All right, in that case, I guess there's no problem, is there? Thank you, Jonah. Ben, say 'thank you' to Mr. Boyd."

"Thank you. Can I go now and decide which poems to read?"

"But we haven't had dessert. And you said 'poem,' not 'poems.'"

"I don't want dessert."

"Just wait until after dessert. Denny?"

Nancy got up and went into the kitchen. I followed.

"Oh, I just don't know about this," she said as she arranged

74

the pumpkin pie on its plate. "I mean, do you think his poetry's any good? I hope Boyd's not expecting some little genius. It's not that I'm not supportive of Ben, it's just—well, you don't follow up a dinner of beef Wellington with Twinkies, do you?"

"I wouldn't worry. It's just a casual thing. And who knows? Maybe Boyd will think Ben *is* a genius, and take him under his wing, and the next thing we know, he'll be the toast of New York."

"Dear Denny, so young and so idealistic," Nancy said, plunging a spoon into a gallon of vanilla ice cream. That shut me up.

The desserts were now ready—in addition to pumpkin pie, banana cream pie, apple pie, and a chocolate pecan pie that Daphne had made. We returned to the dining room, bearing trays piled high with plates as well as the tub of ice cream. Nancy sliced. I scooped.

No one talked much, except to compliment the pies.

"Can I go now?" Ben asked after a few minutes.

"*May* I go now," Nancy corrected. "And yes, you can."

He dashed from the table.

"Well, who's for coffee?" Various hands shot up. Nancy hustled off to make the coffee—Boyd said he would help her—and the rest of us retreated to the study, where Phil went to work arranging chairs, and Ernest set up a makeshift lectern, using a plant stand and a dictionary holder. I sat on the sofa, next to Daphne and Glenn. Anne, holding a fresh glass of wine, had claimed a spot next to Ben, who was sitting on a sort of daybed pushed up against the bookshelves, going through his sheaf of poems. "How you've grown!" she said, tousling

75

his hair. "Remember when you were just a little tyke? I used to give you back rubs."

He didn't answer.

"You used to squirm around and say it tickled, but then you'd relax into it," Anne said, her fingers moving to his shoulders.

"Stop, I'm trying to concentrate."

She laughed. As the evening wore on, her laugh had grown harsher, with an almost granular edge. And now Nancy came in, apronless, and bearing a tray with cups, saucers, and spoons piled on it, followed by Boyd with his four notebooks, the coffee pot, the cream, and the sugar: an accident waiting to happen that, fortunately, didn't. Nancy poured and handed out cups. "Might I just squeeze in?" she asked when she was done, insinuating herself into the narrow space that separated Anne from Ben.

"Be my guest," Anne said. "By the way, Nancy, I love those sheets."

"Oh, thanks."

Daphne rolled her eyes.

"Well, shall we begin?" Ernest ejected Little Hans from the leather rocker and claimed it for himself. "Who goes first?"

"Oh, you, of course, Jonah," Nancy said.

"I don't know, I think my wife is right, we should let youth have its say."

"Or perhaps it should be age before beauty," Anne said, this time laughing so loudly that her laugh turned into a coughing fit.

Giving her a look that might not have been affectionate, Boyd stepped to the lectern, and opened one of his notebooks. "I think I'll simplify matters by reading from the first chapter.

That way I won't have to go through all the rigmarole of explaining who everyone is and what's already happened and so on." He cleared his throat. "By the way, the novel is called *Gonesse*. As our young poet so astutely noted, it is about ballooning. I got the idea from some wallpaper I saw in Paris once—a ballooning *toile de Jouy*." He gazed hard at the notebook. "Oh, and the hero—Agostinelli—was a real person. He was Proust's chauffeur, and probably his lover."

"Interesting," Nancy said.

"All right, Chapter One." Again, Boyd cleared his throat. And then, in that soothing if slightly cracked baritone, he read: "To make love in a balloon . . ."

For all sorts of reasons that will later become obvious, I wish today that I could remember more about that reading. Many years have passed, though, and all that remains with me— aside from a general recollection of the story—is that line. *To make love in a balloon . . .* Already it was clear to me that Boyd, for all his foppishness, was a man who knew how to give pleasure to a woman. Anne had said as much in her letters, and I had seen it for myself, in the ease with which, when Nancy had reached to shake his hand, he had swept her into an embrace. And now here he stood, in the study, a room that had heretofore, for me, held not the slightest erotic connotations, reading aloud a description of his hero, Agostinelli, making love to a French noblewoman in the basket of a balloon five hundred feet above Paris: a splendid and literally panoramic set piece, in which the complex undoing of hasps and petticoats, the arranging of limbs within a confining and in no sense stable space, and the gymnastic difficulties involved in simultaneously keeping the balloon aloft and the woman in ecstasy, are juxtaposed with what seemed to me at the time to be fabulous descriptions of Paris as seen from the air, its waterways and churches, its towers and gargoyles and green patches of park swirling as the balloon gyrates in cold gusts of wind. As he read, Nancy blushed, while over Ernest's face there stole a flush of amusement that intensified whenever our eyes met. I don't think anyone had expected anything like this from Jonah Boyd, and later, I wondered if he had chosen to read that particular scene in order to shock us. *To make love in a balloon . . .* He read for a long time, for what seemed like hours. I didn't get bored. I don't think anyone got bored. Nancy's face was responsive and alert. Ben, too, appeared rapt, as well as oblivious to Anne's fingers, which were now stroking his neck. And then the balloon landed, and the noblewoman, rearranging her layered motley of undergarments, stepped out of the basket and into a waiting *calèche,* and Agostinelli, rather dispiritedly, went off to meet Proust.

Boyd closed the notebook. We applauded. "Oh, that was wonderful, thank you," Nancy said. "You made it all seem so . . . real."

"He did a lot of research," Anne said with more than a touch of pride. "During his Guggenheim year. That was just before we met."

"I hope it doesn't seem—I don't know—too historical novel-ly. You know, with that arid, over-researched, museum-ish kind of air."

"Not at all, not at all," said Ernest. "In fact, if it hadn't been for the sex, and the language, and the present tense, and I hadn't known it was yours, I probably would have assumed that this was written at the same time that it took place."

"Oh, I'm so glad! That's a real compliment. Thank you." Boyd sat down. Then there was a moment of uneasy silence, during which it seemed that something had been forgotten. And of course, what had been forgotten was Ben, who now coughed to remind the assembled of his place in the program. It did the trick. "Well, shall we hear from our young poet now?" Boyd asked.

"Here, here," Phil Perry seconded.

Ben stepped up to the lectern. There was in his eyes a mixture of vitality and anxiety the likes of which I'd never before seen him exhibit. Little did I know how much that moment meant to him!

As for Nancy, from the instant Ben ascended, her back went rigid, and all pleasure drained from her face. She arranged her hands carefully in her lap. "He looks so handsome," Anne whispered too loudly. "But he needs to work on his posture! Tennis would help."

In imitation of Boyd, Ben cleared his throat. "Thank you," he said. "I'm now going to read to you a poem called 'Vancouver.' It is dedicated to my brother, Mark Allen Wright."

Nancy blanched. I could almost hear the words "Oh no" escape her lips.

Today I have the poem in front of me. Ben gave me a copy a few months before he died, at my request. It is a long poem, loosely based on "The Waste Land," which at the time he was in the process of memorizing. It begins (and Ben began, that Thanksgiving):

> April is not the cruellest month.
> The cruellest month is July—

There was a sound, I thought, of stifled laughter, though I couldn't tell where it came from. Ben glanced up. Then he

79

returned his attention to the page. It seemed he had lost his place, so he started again.

> April is not the cruellest month.
> The cruellest month is July,
> Bringer of drought or deluge,
> Gray rainy afternoons when brothers leave.

A startled look crossed Ernest's face. I don't think it had ever occurred to him that during all those weeks, the long drama of Mark's exile, his younger son might actually have been listening; taking in every word.

Ben read on. The poem is very long, and divided into four sections, the first concerning (mostly) Southern California summer, and rainlessness, and "my father's hose nosing soil / The thirst of which is never slaked." Much metaphorical fuss is made, in the second section, over the Datsun's lack of a reverse gear:

> As if in kidnapping him
> It was promising a one-way journey
> From which he would never come back.

In another line, Ben writes that "Assuming there were no delays / They would arrive in Vancouver on time." (That sort of redundancy, I am sorry to say, was typical of his poetry.) Part three brings the travelers to San Francisco, where they stop for the night, and encounter some rather ill-tempered mermen off of Aquatic Park. It turns out that they are suicides who jumped off the Golden Gate Bridge:

We are the dead, we are the lost,
We are the mer-people of San Francisco Bay!
Entwined by seaweed, scales climb up our arms.
We watch for the next body to fall, always eager
To add another to our tribe!

At last, in part four, the travelers arrive in Vancouver. That
Ben had at this point never visited the city, and knew nothing
of its geography, seems not to have been any kind of deterrent
to him in describing a rather fantastic landscape of hills and
lakes and bridges, the sole occupants of which, apparently, are
draft dodgers who spend their days staring through telescopes
across the border at an America going about its business
without regard to the suffering of its exiled sons:

In the supermarket, the housewives
Load their carts with canned cranberry sauce,
Canned pumpkin, canned gravy, frozen turkeys,
At school the children cut turkeys
Out of construction paper,
Make turkeys from clay,
Turkeys from papier-mâché . . .

The poem concludes with a scene of such bathos that even
the memory of its being read makes me grimace. In a bizarre
ceremony that defies all laws of realism, brothers shake hands
across a national frontier as clearly demarcated as a child's
drawing of the Berlin wall:

Ignoring the frowning guards,
He holds out his arm

And I take his hand, and in that squeeze there is
Defiance of unjust laws, and a refusal to weaken.
I wish I could pull him across to me, but I know
That if I did, he would be shot.
And so I stay where I am,
Until he lets go, and walks
Sadly back into Vancouver.
Behind me Mother weeps.
We stay until he is out of sight,
And then we go home.

Ben stepped back. "Thank you," he said. I looked around myself. To my amazement, Jonah Boyd began to applaud. And then Nancy applauded too, furiously, and Ernest, and Daphne, and then everyone else. I don't know whether they were simply following Boyd's lead, or responding to some imaginative vigor that the poem revealed, a vigor of which, curiously enough, its imprecision and ragged sentimentality and obliviousness to all rules of structure and concerns about accuracy might have been the ultimate proof. For there is this to be said about "Vancouver": Bombastic though it is, there is life in the thing. Alas Ben's refusal, as always, to accept (much less contend with) the interfering laws imposed by logic, form, and the real world in the end shipwrecks him, rendering the poem, like all his poems, unpublishable and probably unreadable. But that didn't matter to his audience on Thanksgiving eve 1969. After all, he was only fifteen. What they saw was an unsuspected promise, albeit one which it would take him many long years to fulfill.

The applause died out—and then, to my surprise, Anne was the first to stand. "Ben, that was wonderful, just wonderful," she said, stumbling up to him and taking him in an embrace that opened Nancy's mouth, as there was in it more than a touch of salaciousness. Anne's breasts were squashed flat against his chest; she might have been grinding her hips. I wasn't sure. In any case, Boyd saved the day. "Yes, wasn't it?" he echoed, taking his wife's hand and leading her back to the daybed, away from Ben. "Very exciting. Have you sent it to your brother?"

"No."

"I think you should," Nancy said. "Mark will be thrilled. Moved."

"I don't want him to read it until it's published," Ben said. "I've sent it to *The New Yorker*."

"Oh, *The New Yorker*! If there's one thing I admire in a young writer, it's gumption. I myself stopped sending stories to *The New Yorker* fifteen years ago. I figured, after Bill Maxwell had turned down thirty-five of them, what was the point in wasting any more postage?"

"Oh, Jonah, don't worry, Ben doesn't *really* expect *The New Yorker* to publish his poem," Nancy said.

"Yes, I do."

"No matter . . . If they do, it'll be wonderful, and if they don't, it'll be even more wonderful." She clapped her hands together, apparently unfazed by the utter pointlessness of this remark. "Well, hasn't this been a wonderful evening? And now who's ready for more pie?"

"I thought maybe I could read a second poem," Ben said.

"Now, Ben, one's enough. We don't want to tire Mr. Boyd. After all, he and Anne have had a very long day. They had to get up very early in the morning on the East Coast, which is the middle of the night here."

"But I only want to read one more!"

Unfortunately for Ben the crowd was already dispersing, moving back toward the kitchen. "Sorry, honey," Nancy said, and rested her hand on her son's head.

He flinched it away. "It's not fair," he said.

"What's not? You had your chance."

"But I only read half as long as he did."

"Well, Mr. Boyd's a famous novelist. When you're a famous poet, you can read twice as long, how about that?"

"I'll tell you what, Ben," Boyd interjected. "How about if we go off somewhere and *I* listen to some more of your poems?"

"Oh, Jonah, you don't have to do that . . ."

"But I want to. Really, I think it's my duty, as an old gorgon of a writer, to impart what wisdom I possess to this young acolyte."

"But you must be tired . . ."

"I'm not."

"Let them," Anne said.

Ben looked pleadingly into Nancy's eyes. She hesitated. "Are you sure?"

Boyd rested a hand on Ben's shoulder. "I'm absolutely sure."

"Okay . . . But Ben, you have to promise not to keep Mr. Boyd longer than he feels like listening."

"Let's go to your room."

"What about your room?"

"Ben, you have to promise."

"I promise, okay?" And he led Boyd off. Chin cupped in hand, Nancy watched them recede, until Anne touched her on the shoulder. She turned. Anne smiled at her friend, for the first time that evening, with what looked like affection.

"I've had a wonderful time," she said.

"Have you? I'm so glad!"

Anne leaned in closer, so close that Nancy must have been able to smell the gin on her breath. "Listen, I know it's late . . . but what would you say to a little Mozart?"

Nancy's eyes brightened. "Really?"

"Really."

"May we listen?" asked Phil Perry.

"You will hear in any case," Anne said. "Whether you choose to listen is up to you."

Phil took the cue, and followed them into the living room, where he sat down on the sofa. I sat next to him. And so the reading was followed by a recital the decided mediocrity and unmusicality of which, I was gratified to hear, was not to be explained away by mere lack of practice. Magical harmonies indeed! Another small, if private, victory for me, on that night that was to be marked by so many losses.

Seven

EVEN TODAY I don't like to think about Phil Perry. But he plays a role in this story, and so I suppose I don't have any choice. What have I said so far? That he was one of Ernest's Ph.D. students, that he was scrawny, that he ate a lot. To which I can add: He was prone to intense, one-sided crushes on girls whom he would persist in bothering long after they had told him to get lost. (In modern parlance, a stalker.) He liked to boast that his IQ was 180, and that he was a member of MENSA—mostly, he claimed, because it was a good place to meet girls. Glenn often made fun of him. Although in theory they were friends, and worked together under Ernest on a number of projects, I always suspected that in his heart Phil hated Glenn, and envied him, since Glenn had so much more success with women. Also academically, Glenn was the more successful of the pair. Phil was a kind of genius, possessed of a rare instinct and passion for his subject, but he lacked Glenn's self-discipline and savoir-faire. He didn't know how to dress or smile. Nor had he mastered the art, as Glenn had, of giving little Christmas gifts to the wife of the boss, or flirting with his secretary. His papers were inspired and chaotic and might have been great, had he been able to finish them.

But he never could, and so his transcript was full of incompletes. We all liked Phil, and felt sorry for him. But we adored Glenn.

Glenn was handsome. He had curly auburn hair that bleached blond in the summer, and wide eyes that he set off by wearing tiny wire-rimmed glasses. No one knows this, but I had an affair with him in the months just after Daphne left him, when he had been turned down for tenure at Wellspring but had yet to find another job. As a lover he displayed the same qualities of flash and eagerness to please, as well as the slight whiff of pandering, that marked his academic career. Such an appeal, however, gets dull in a fairly short order. I think what galled Phil was the impression, personified in Glenn, that the slick and the mediocre will always win out over the clumsy and the brilliant. Glenn's failure to get tenure was an intellectual vindication from which Phil might have taken comfort, had he only shown a little more patience.

Whenever Phil and Glenn were in the house together with Ernest, there was a palpable tension in the air. This was because Ernest played them off each other—for their own good, he insisted. I suppose he imagined that by flaunting his preference for Glenn, he might ignite in Phil some healthy competitive spirit, induce him to pull up his bootstraps and develop a manner to match his talents. But it never happened. Phil continued to stumble along, no doubt vexed by the favoritism that Ernest showed Glenn—for example, by confiding in him, that Thanksgiving, the fascinating episode of Jonah Boyd "misplacing" his notebooks. Ernest and Glenn worked together in interrogating Boyd, they made a spectacle of their alliance as mentor and disciple, which Phil was forced to witness, all the while trying to fill in the blanks for himself.

Had I been more observant, I might have seen early signs of the envy that would erupt so many years later in violence—but at the time there was so much else to keep track of, I ended up more or less ignoring Phil. As I usually did. As everyone usually did.

Two hours after the readings ended—the kitchen cleaned, Glenn and Phil gone, and the Boyds put to bed—I climbed into my notoriously bad-tempered Dodge Dart, turned the key in the ignition, and found that it would not start.

Cursing, I returned to the kitchen. Nancy was sitting at the tulip table in her bathrobe, smoking a cigarette and thumbing rather listlessly through the recipe pages of *Sunset*.

She looked up. "What are you doing back here?" she asked.

"The car won't start."

"Oh, how annoying. Ernest!"

He too was in his bathrobe. Together, we went outside to look under the hood.

"Nothing wrong that I can see," Ernest said, slipping his hand down the back of my skirt. "But then again, I'm no mechanic."

"I'll call a taxi."

"No need for a taxi. I can drive you home." He started to kiss me.

"Wouldn't it be simpler if Denny just stayed the night here?" Nancy called from the kitchen door. "She can sleep with Daphne on the fold-out bed in the study. And that way she'll be here in the morning when the tow truck comes."

Ernest withdrew his hand. In the dark, had she seen?

"That's probably a better plan," he said, moving away from me into the moonlight.

Back indoors, Nancy led me to the study, the door to which

she simultaneously rapped on and pushed open. "Daphne, Denny's car's broken down, so she's going to bunk with you . . . Oh." Daphne was not in bed; she was sitting at the table near the window, in jeans and a sweater set, putting on makeup.

"Can't you wait for a person to say 'Come in'?" she asked.

"Sorry," Nancy said. "Listen, I'm exhausted. Be a sweetheart and show Denny where the extra towels are, will you?" As if in compensation for her earlier brusqueness, she patted Daphne's head rather as she might have Little Hans's. "Well, good night, girls. And thanks again for all your help today."

"Nancy—"

"What?"

"Are you happy how things turned out? I mean, seeing Anne?"

"Oh, delighted, delighted." But her smile was weary. "Of course, I have to admit, the drinking worries me . . . Well, no need to think about that now. Try and get a good night's sleep."

She left, closing the door softly.

I sat on the daybed. "So," I said to Daphne, "I'll bet you weren't expecting to have a roommate tonight, were you?"

Daphne had resumed her makeup. "I wasn't, actually."

I took off one shoe. "Going out?"

She turned to face me. "Can I trust you? You're younger than my parents. I hope I can trust you."

"Of course you can."

She leaned closer. "The fact is, I do have plans tonight— only they're ones I don't want anyone to find out about. You see, for some time now—a few months—I've been involved with someone, and for all sorts of reasons, for the time being at least, we need to keep it quiet—"

89

"You mean Glenn."

She raised her eyebrows in surprise. "You mean you knew?"

"Well, if you'll pardon my saying so, it wouldn't take a rocket scientist—"

"Oh, but do you think that means my parents have guessed? Because if my dad found out, it could be awful for Glenn. Dad wouldn't approve. The age difference and all, and the fact that Glenn's his sort of, you know, protégé."

"I don't think your father knows. You mother, on the other hand—well, you may have noticed that she didn't even ask you why you were putting on makeup at eleven o'clock at night."

"Dear mother. She can be so—well, you know, *difficult* sometimes, and then sometimes she can sense something, and be totally cool without even saying a word." Suddenly Daphne jumped up and sat next to me on the daybed. "Oh, Denny, I had no idea you were so cool! Do you have a boyfriend? I hope you don't mind my asking."

"I've had several. At the moment . . . No, not at the moment."

"That's too bad. But here's the thing. Your having to stay here tonight—it's put me in sort of an awkward position."

"Why? Is Glenn coming over?"

"God, no! I couldn't ever—you know—right here in the house, with Mother and Father on the other side of the wall. Yuck! No, the plan is, he's going to pick me up at midnight, across the street. And we're going back to his apartment. And then at five, before anyone's up, he'll drop me off, and I'll get into bed. Oh, you will help us out, won't you, and not say anything?"

90

"Don't worry," I said. "The last thing I'd want to do is interrupt the course of young love." I patted her hand. "Go. Have fun. I won't say a word."

Relief filled Daphne's eyes. "Oh, Denny, you really are wonderful. I never would have thought you could be that cool!" She removed my hand from hers. "Listen, I'd better scoot. And when I get back, don't scream or anything. I'll be as quiet as I can."

"No problem."

She opened the door. "Oh, and you can borrow my night gown if you want. It's clean. Bye."

She tiptoed out, shutting the door behind her so slowly that it groaned—a louder noise by far than the click of quick closure. From the kitchen where he was sleeping, Little Hans gave a yelp. There was a whispered curse. Another door opened, and shut again.

I took off my other shoe. I listened for—and thought I heard, very far off—the sound of a car turning the curve.

Then I was alone.

I looked around. Never before in the years I'd known them had I slept in the Wrights' house. Now, rubbing my stocking feet into the carpet, I marveled at a certain quality of cushioned silence that it radiated, a warm, dozing purr, as if somewhere in the midst of that rich layering of rugs and books and paintings and mirrors a cat lay hidden, and was taking pleasure in cleaning itself. This was the sound—the protective, lulling melody—of affluence, and perhaps only those, like me, whom affluence admits only as visitors can name it. It was hard to believe that just a few feet away, just on the other side of a none-too-thick wall, Nancy and Ernest were going through their bedtime rituals. And what did those rituals consist of? Did Nancy wear curlers? Did Ernest stuff his ears with cotton? Did they make love? The last seemed unlikely. Even so, as I took off my clothes, I made a little striptease out of my disrobing, swinging my stockings in the air, imagining as my audience . . . who? Ernest? Nancy?

It didn't matter. No sooner was I down to my underwear than shame overtook me, and I bundled myself into Daphne's nightgown, which was flannel, patterned with teddy bears in nightcaps, and much too small. I opened the sofa bed, which was already made, switched off the lamp, and snuggled under the covers. But from outside moonlight penetrated through the windows, over which, as it happened, I had neglected to draw the curtains, and I could not sleep. Nor could I muster the energy to climb out of bed and make the room dark; or take the battery out of the wall clock, the persistent ticking of which I felt as a steady thud just beneath my diaphragm. And so I lay awake, listening for noises, and hearing some—several knocks, a not very loud crash, as of something being dropped. A toilet flushed. What time was it? One? Two? I had no idea.

The darkness settled. I thought about the first Thanksgiving I'd spent with the Wrights, the long night afterward during which I'd actually convinced myself that they'd invited me only to make me the subject of some strange social experiment. Now I understood that their motives for embracing me were not only more complex than I had suspected, but individual: Nancy needed me to be a failure, Ernest needed me as an alternative to Nancy . . . and now Daphne seemed to need me to be her confidante. She was a difficult girl to read, her expression as opaque as her flat, bland hair. I had no idea if she liked me. Come to think of it, I had no idea if she liked anybody. Most of the time she projected a façade of indifference to the rest of the world—and then there would be those occasional flashes of rebelliousness, or rage, or even tenderness. Also a certain hardness: The implacability to which Nancy could merely aspire, Daphne, at seventeen, had already mastered. There was no question as to who would win *that* war. Nor did it surprise me that Glenn loved her: The challenge was getting through the carapace, reaching the pearl of sweetness within—and to that quest, I have discovered, some men are more than willing to devote their lives.

Well, she was gone now—presumably off at Glenn's apartment, which, as it happened, was in the complex next to mine: Springwell, locus of all fulfillments the necessity of which Florizona Avenue proscribed. As I lay on the sofa bed, the faces of the Wrights seemed to float above me, like the winged, disembodied heads of seraphim. Despite my wakefulness, I felt extraordinarily content; and indeed, at some point I must have dropped off, because when, just before dawn, Daphne came in, I did scream, despite my promise not to. No one woke, though—or at least, I heard no one wake. All night the walls and the window frames had been creaking, as if to protest the extra weight the house was being forced to bear, all these bodies shifting in sleep. Now Daphne stripped down to her bra and panties and climbed in next to me. Her hair smelled of smoke.

"Oh, Denny, what a night it's been," she said.

"Has it?"

Her lips were as close to mine as a lover's. "Glenn was furious that I told you about us. He's terribly worried that you'll tell my father. I tried to reassure him, but you know how men are. They won't listen."

"I know."

"Oh, but after that . . . May I tell you? I've got to tell someone. You see, tonight Glenn asked me . . . Well, he didn't exactly ask me, but he broached the subject . . . I mean, getting married."

"Married! But you're only seventeen!"

"Oh, not now! In the future, after I've graduated . . . because, you see, it looks very likely—don't tell anyone this, because it isn't official yet—it looks like the department's going to offer Glenn a job. Dad doesn't want word to get around because he's afraid it will upset Phil—you know, that Glenn is getting an offer and he isn't. And if Glenn gets the job, and he gets tenure—well, that means that down the road, we can have the house."

"What house?"

"This house, of course! It's always been Mother's hope that one of us could keep it after she and Dad—you know—pass away. You know how she feels about the place, how important it is to her that it stay in the family. But this way—if Glenn gets the job—the problem's solved."

"But all that's so far in the future! Twenty, thirty years. Are you really thinking that far ahead, at your age?"

"It's not *that* far ahead! Besides, soon enough, Dad will want to retire. They'll want a smaller place." Daphne lay back, besotted by her own vision. "There's so much I'd do if this house were ours! For a start, paint the kitchen. And fill in that stupid barbecue pit." She propped herself up on one elbow. "Oh, Denny, I don't know how well you know Glenn, but he's really the most wonderful . . . so smart and insightful. And an amazing lover. I mean, he really knows how to fuck—oh, have I shocked you?"

"Of course not."

"Good." Daphne sounded disappointed. "Tonight was the most marvelous night. May I tell you about it?"

"Sure," I said. "Tell me everything."

"Okay," she said.

And then, for almost an hour, until the sun coming through the windows roused Dora to yowl for her breakfast, she did.

Eight

THAT MORNING NANCY hustled me out of bed early. As it turned out, she had already called a tow truck for my car, and it was on its way. I only had time to guzzle down a cup of coffee and ask that she give the Boyds, who were still in bed, my regards, before the truck arrived; with great speed and dexterity, the driver hooked my poor car to its tail, like some enormous fish. At last I climbed into the cab, and he gazed at me in frank bemusement: a woman wearing last night's makeup, in a wrinkled blouse and too formal skirt. He gave me his phone number, though, and proposed that I call him if I had any free time over the weekend.

For the rest of the day the logistics of auto repair consumed me. The world shrunk to a narrow island consisting of my apartment at one end and at the other the local Dodge dealership, with only a stretch of freeway I had no means of navigating in between. Gaskets, oil filters, and catalytic converters became the stuff not only of my conscious life but of my dreams. I had trouble sleeping; even wearing earplugs I could not block out the noise of the freeway—an invasive noise, so different from the soothing hum of Florizona Avenue. The dishwasher was noisy too; everything in that apartment was gimcrack, assaultive, and I woke up in the morning with a headache. I wanted breakfast, and had no food. I wanted to get out, and couldn't, which was probably why, when Nancy phoned around ten-thirty, I could barely contain my delight. "I'm sorry to bother you," she said, "I know you're busy with your car, but I need some help. Can you come over? I'll pay for a taxi."

"Of course," I said, trying not to sound too overjoyed. "But what's wrong?"

Something crunched in background. "It's better if I explain once you're here. It's really quite—oops, I'd better go. Oh, and Denny—thanks."

I arrived half an hour later. Nancy was on her knees at the foot of the staircase that climbed to the kitchen, rifling through the contents of an overturned garbage can.

"I got here as fast as I could," I said. "But what are you doing?"

"Oh, hi." She was inserting a rubber-gloved hand into the morass of turkey parts and soiled paper towels. "I'm really so glad you're here, Denny. I'm afraid there's been some trouble."

"What happened?"

"Jonah Boyd's lost his notebooks."

"But I thought they were leaving this morning."

"They did leave. Two hours ago. But then about an hour after that, I got this frantic phone call from Anne. They were on the interstate, and they'd pulled over at a rest plaza. It seems that once again Jonah had one of his feelings, just like on the way from the airport, and so they pulled over to make sure the notebooks were still in his briefcase. And they weren't."

"Oh, no. Where could he have left them?"

"That's just it, no one knows. They might be here in the house, or they might not. Because yesterday he took Ben down to the arroyo, and he definitely had the notebooks with him then. And then we all met up at a Chinese restaurant—they came in the rental car, Ernest and I drove Anne from the house—and he might have had them there, too. The problem is, he can't remember when he last saw them. It's so exasperating! Oh, what's this?" She fished out a box that had contained some frozen Parker House rolls. "No, nothing here."

"But they shouldn't be that hard to find. I mean, there are four of them, and they're not small. Have you called the Chinese restaurant?"

"They don't open until five."

"What can I do?"

"If you could just help Ernest out in the study . . . Daphne's doing her room, and Ben his. The Boyds have turned around and are going to do the arroyo. I've told everyone to adopt this system I saw on television, where you divide each area into quadrants and go quadrant by quadrant. A woman found a lost diamond earring that way."

Having put the garbage can to rights, we went inside, where I found Ernest in the study, removing the cushions from the daybed. A piece of popcorn, I saw, had lodged in one of the corners.

"Nancy told me what happened," I said. "Any luck so far?"

"No, and there's not going to be," Ernest said. "And you know why? Because they're not here."

"How do you know?"

"Isn't it obvious? They're in some Dumpster, or burned up in the incinerator behind the Chinese restaurant. Who cares?

The point is, if he's lost them, it's because he wanted to lose them. Textbook parapraxis."

From typing Ernest's correspondence, I was familiar with the term, if not this particular usage. "But I thought *parapraxis* meant letting something slip that you didn't mean to say," I said.

"Yes, but it can also mean answering a question wrong on a test because you secretly want to fail. Or losing something"— he formed his fingers into quotation marks—" 'accidentally on purpose.' "

"And you think that's what happened with Boyd?"

"There's no question. Consider that twice already—that we know of—he's been saved just in the nick of time 'thanks to the intervention of the muse,' or some such nonsense. I mean, you don't just keep losing things, and losing them, and never take any precautions, unless on some level you're really hoping to lose them. Or because you get your kicks from the risk, the danger."

"But a novel—something he's been working on for years—"

"For all we know, the bit he read us is all there is, the rest of the notebooks are blank. Or think about it this way: You're betting everything you've got on one book, and one day you wake up and realize it's just not very good. Then what do you do? If it's lost, no one will ever be able to criticize it. It will never be a failure. It'll exist in some sort of ideal state for all eternity, as a 'lost masterpiece.' Of course, that's a pretty desperate tactic, and not one, I suspect, that any normal person would opt for consciously—but from the point of view of the subconscious, it makes perfect sense."

Nancy came in. "What are you two doing just standing there and gabbing?" she said. "We've still got the living room to do."

"Relax. There's no need. They're not going to turn up." Ernest replaced the cushions on the daybed. "As head of this household, I hereby declare this search over."

"But if we haven't looked—"

"There's no point. Give it up."

Ernest went outside, to his office.

"He doesn't like Boyd," Nancy said, getting down on her knees to peer under a table.

"Why not?"

"All that talk about the muse got on his nerves. Also, he didn't appreciate what Boyd read. He said it was pornographic."

Ben slunk through the door. "Nothing in my room. Daphne's still looking in hers."

The bell rang. "Oh no," Nancy said. "Who on earth could that be? I hope it's not—"

But it was. Opening the kitchen door, Nancy admitted the Boyds. Anne looked—if this was possible—even more rumpled than she had upon her arrival from the airport. As for Jonah Boyd, he wore on his pallid face an expression of mute resignation—as if he had fast-forwarded through panic, false hope, and anger, and now stood on the brink of a premature acceptance.

Anne was not in anywhere near so calm a state. "Any luck?" she asked, shimmying out of her ratty coat.

"Oh, Annie, I'm sorry, not yet. How about on your end?"

"None." She sat heavily at the tulip table. "Although we left a description with the police, and they've promised to keep an eye open down at the arroyo. We went by the Chinese restaurant, too. They weren't open. I tried to get into their Dumpster but it was locked."

"My wife is indefatigable," Boyd said with great fatigue. "She would climb into Dumpsters on my behalf."

"Jonah, why don't you sit down, too? Would you like some coffee?"

"Thank you." He eased himself into a chair. "And thank you—all of you—for helping out. It's rather embarrassing, what's happened."

"Now there's nothing to be embarrassed about. Anyway, all we've done is what any friend would do. We've looked. I'm just sorry nothing's shown up—yet."

"Well, don't trouble yourselves too much. This is no one's fault but my own. Oh, hello," he said to Ben, who had just wandered into the kitchen. "And how is your new poem coming along, young man? The one about the sea elephants—"

Anne hit herself on the forehead. "Are you completely mad? Do you live in a dream world?"

"No, I do not. Thank you, Nancy." (She had just handed him a mug of coffee.) "I simply fail to see, lady wife, why ordinary life has to stop completely just because there's been a slight setback."

Anne buried her face in her hands. "This is the end," she said. "And what are you supposed to do now? Return the advance to the publisher? In that case, we'll be broke. We'll have to sell the house."

"Oh, Anne," Nancy said, "I'm sure it won't come to that."

"And you're coming up for tenure. Without a book, what are you going to tell the chair? This is supposed to be your breakthrough novel, remember, the one that's going to make us rich. Good God, it's the end of everything."

"Now look," Nancy said, "there's no need to be so negative. We've hardly begun to look. We just have to be calm and methodical, and Jonah, maybe you need to try to retrace your steps. To work at remembering—to the best of your ability—the last time you were *sure* you had the notebooks."

"You had them at the arroyo," Ben said. "I remember seeing them on the bench."

"But did I have them when we got up to leave? That's the question."

"I think you did."

"Or at the Chinese restaurant. Does anyone remember seeing them at the Chinese restaurant?"

A vague shaking of heads greeted this question. No one could remember.

"What about yesterday morning, when you were out in the backyard with Ben?"

"That's right. We sat down in that very odd barbecue pit."

"But that was before we went to the arroyo," Ben reminded, "and you had them at the arroyo."

"Oh, so I did," Boyd said. "So I did."

A silence fell. "Well, the police here are very good," Nancy said after a moment. "I'm sure you can count on them."

"And when does the Chinese restaurant open?"

"Five, I think."

She looked at the clock. It was half past noon.

I could tell from her expression that the prospect of having the Boyds on her hands until five, watching the clock, was more than she could stomach. So I said, "Maybe at this point we'd do best to head back over to the arroyo ourselves, and do a more careful search."

"I don't know how much ground is left to cover," Boyd said. "We checked all around the bench where Ben and I sat, not to mention in the garbage cans, and there was nothing."

"Still, it couldn't hurt to have a fresh pair of eyes. I don't have anything. I'm waiting for my car. I'd be glad to help. And I'm sure Ben would too—wouldn't you, Ben?"

"Why not?"

"Oh, well, if you think that's a good idea," said Nancy, the relief in her voice audible, at least to me. "Unless, of course, you'd prefer just to wait here, in which case I could make some lunch . . ."

"No, no," Anne said. "I think the last thing we want to be doing is just sitting around. I, for one, would rather be on my hands and knees in the bushes, digging."

I stood. "Well, shall we go, then?"

"We can take the rental car," Boyd said, standing too.

And then the four of us shuffled out the back door.

Nothing turned up at the arroyo. We spent about two hours scouring the bushes around and behind the bench on which Boyd and Ben had sat, and also around several other benches, in case they had gotten the benches mixed up. Anne sifted through every trash can, while Boyd and Ben dug through the carpet of fallen leaves that blanketed the ground. They seemed to work happily together, and not for the last time, I wondered what kind of bond could have united this pair, a successful novelist of middle age and the teenage author of some pretentious verse. Perhaps Boyd really had seen in Ben's writing a germ of raw talent that he thought worth cultivating. Or perhaps the connection was sentimental, the fruit of a longing, on Boyd's part, for a son, and Ben's for a father—understandable, given that at this stage Ernest paid practically no attention at all to Ben, while Boyd hardly ever had the chance to see his children, who lived with their mother in Dallas. In any case, they had spent the better part of the weekend sequestered together, first in Ben's room, and then in the barbecue pit, and then here at the arroyo, caught up in an orgy of reading and talking at some point during which (maybe) Boyd had stood up and walked away without his notebooks. They remained pregnantly behind, covers opening to reveal gold-edged, cream-colored tongues that called out in inaudible voices not to be abandoned, as the little tin soldier had called out as he went down the drain: *au secours* . . . And meanwhile Anne Boyd patiently made her way through the contents of yet another trash can: crumpled paper bags, banana peels, used rubbers, sheets of newspaper smeared with dog shit, a dirty sock . . .

After about two hours we gave up. We had a rather late and unhappy lunch at the Pie 'n Burger, during which Anne said almost nothing and ate with surprising animation, while Boyd ate almost nothing and spent practically the whole time talking with Ben about poetry. I paid the bill, confident that Nancy would want me to, and offer to reimburse me. Then we headed over to the Chinese restaurant, where as luck would have it, the cook was just opening the front door. Because he spoke almost no English, explaining to him what had happened proved to be a frustratingly protracted enterprise, in the course of which Boyd was forced to resort to the tired device of drawing out his misadventures as a kind of comic strip. Fortunately the hostess soon arrived, a snappy and efficient woman who remembered Boyd from the night before and assured him almost before he had asked that he had left nothing behind. Nothing was in the cloak room, or the kitchen. Nor would she and her staff have ever allowed any items so obviously left by customers to be thrown in the trash. It took all the calming influence that Boyd and I could muster to dissuade Anne from forcing the poor woman to unlock the Dumpster so that she could climb into it. Eventually, however, she must have been convinced that there was nothing further to be learned at the Chinese restaurant, for she thanked the hostess, and drifted out the door. Boyd thanked the hostess as well, and tried to give her a tip, which she refused. He left his phone number and asked that she call him if anything should turn up. Then we all turned around and followed Anne to the parking lot.

We drove in silence back to the Wrights' house. "Any luck?" Nancy asked eagerly as she opened the kitchen door for us, then—seeing the answer in our faces—tightened her smile into a line and went to make coffee. The Boyds stayed another half hour before heading off to Big Sur in their rented red Chevrolet. Anne was no longer frantic. Waving good-bye, we promised to call if we heard anything from the police, or if anything showed up at the house. But I think at this point we all felt fairly certain that the notebooks were gone for good.

It was nearly dinnertime. Rather gloomily, Nancy set out bread, mustard, mayonnaise, and lettuce. Ernest sliced leftover turkey. We made sandwiches for ourselves. Ben, to my surprise, did not toast his bread—and then Ernest, Ben, Daphne, and I sat down at the tulip table and watched the evening news, which seemed oddly comforting under the circumstances. Only Nancy could not rest. While we ate, she ricocheted around the kitchen, opening cupboards and drawers and peering inside them, until Ernest shouted, "Will you stop that? You're not going to find his goddamn novel in the cutlery drawer."

"I'm not looking for his novel," Nancy replied. "I'm looking for the blue bowl I use for potato salad."

"But we're not having any potato salad."

She turned to the television. More news of the war. "I wonder where the Boyds are now," she said, as if to herself. "Do you think anyone will ever find the notebooks?"

"No."

"Ernest, don't be such a pessimist! Anne seemed so sad. To be perfectly honest, I'm worried about her."

"If you ask me, she's been hysterical from the get-go. Leaving Clifford Armstrong like that—not the behavior of a well-adjusted adult woman."

"But Ben and Jonah Boyd certainly hit it off. Didn't you, Ben?"

"I guess."

"Did he read you more of his novel?"

"Yes."

"And was it as good as what he read aloud on Thanksgiving?"

"I guess."

"Oh, it seems so awful, to lose something like that. Like losing a child, almost . . . I don't know what I'd do if it were me. Maybe he can reconstruct it, from memory."

"A four-hundred-page novel? I don't think so."

"Don't be fooled," Ernest said. "What people get, most of the time, is what they want."

The phone rang. Nancy hurried to answer it. "Oh, Mark," she said, her voice rising with a mixture of pleasure and fear she seemed barely able to contain. "Honey, are you all right? Is something the matter?"

Suddenly Ben was on his feet. "Let me talk to him," he begged, grabbing his mother's arm.

"Just a second, Ben! Your brother wants to talk to you. Hold on! Honey, what's wrong? How was the Thanksgiving?"

Daphne and I cleared the table. As he was wont to do when he thought no one was looking, Ernest winked at me. The turkey carcass, from which several meals had already been scraped, lay bony and denuded on its platter, surrounded by trembling flakes of gelatinized juice. Perhaps Nancy would boil it for broth, before throwing it into the trash she had earlier searched so patiently and so fruitlessly. In any case, she would get rid of it. No one wanted to look at the thing anymore. And then she would return to her piano and her crowned heads, and I would pick up my car. Daphne and Glenn would make love in his apartment. Ben would write another poem.

You see, for most of us, I could envision a future. Even for Ben I could envision a future. And yet for the life of me I could not envision what was going on inside that red Chevrolet.

I put on my coat. "I'm taking Denny home," Ernest suddenly announced to his wife, who either didn't hear him or elected not to answer him, so caught up was she in her conversation with Mark, and in pushing Ben off her arm.

That is as much as I knew of what happened that Thanksgiving, and as much as I would know—for almost thirty years.

Nine

THE NEXT SATURDAY morning I went, as usual, to play with Nancy. She didn't mention Anne's name once. During the week the ersatz guest room had been dismantled, Daphne's frog figurines and stuffed animals and peace sign poster returned to their rightful places.

Nancy didn't speak of Anne the Saturday after that, either, which was odd only in that during the months leading up to Thanksgiving she had spoken of little else. She was now preoccupied with Christmas, a holiday from which, at the Wright house, we strays were excluded as vociferously as at Thanksgiving we were welcomed. As Ben later explained to me, Christmas at 302 Florizona Avenue involved a sequence of private rituals in which each member of the family was required to play a specific role (Ben was the "elf"), all leading up to the climactic unwrapping of the presents, after which the rest of the day was pure letdown. Of course, that Christmas was to be like no other due to Mark's absence, and though Nancy tried to put a brave face on things, I could tell that she was having a hard time. I myself spent Christmas alone. I went to the movies. And then it was New Year's Eve (I spent most of *that* holiday in the backseat of a chemistry professor's car), and the seventies. On Saturdays Nancy and I played, on

Sundays Ernest visited me at my apartment. I stopped thinking about the Boyds, who, to the extent that they still existed for me, did so behind a sort of blackout curtain, and not merely because Nancy and Ernest, so far as I could tell, no longer talked to them; also because what had happened—a loss, despite what Nancy had said, not nearly so terrible as that of a child, but terrible enough—placed them outside any realm of experience that I could touch. Of course, I knew they went on in their exile; they had to go on. What I didn't know was what that going on felt like.

Sometimes a letter or a birthday card arrived from Anne. Then Nancy would shake her head and say, "Remember that awful Thanksgiving? Afterward, for weeks, I kept hoping I'd find the damn notebooks, even when it became eminently clear that I never would." From contacts in Bradford, Nancy learned that in the wake of losing his novel, Boyd had stopped writing. "They say he's put off his tenure vote," she told me. "No one ever sees him—or Anne." One afternoon in 1972 he was killed. In the midst of a blinding rainstorm, he crashed his car into the wall of the abandoned coffin factory. He had been on his way to the liquor store. "And is it any wonder?" Nancy asked. "I mean, imagine it. You work and work on something, you hold it close to your heart, and then one day—poof—it's gone. And to make matters worse, you can't blame anyone but yourself. No wonder he started drinking again. Oh, I just wish it hadn't happened in my house."

"Dr. Wright thinks Boyd lost them on purpose," I reminded her—rather coldly, yet there is consolation to be gained from such knowledge. For those of us on the outside, disaster courted is less threatening than disaster stumbled upon, since pathologies only imply holes in the psyche, whereas accidents

. . . well, they imply holes in the universe, and who's to say you won't be the next one to fall through?

After Boyd's death, for a brief time, Nancy was once again in regular contact with Anne. They spoke several times by telephone; there was even, for a while, talk of Anne flying out for a visit, though this trip never got beyond the planning stages, mostly because Anne refused to be pinned down to a specific date. Eventually Nancy gave up on trying to persuade her, after which the phone conversations became less and less frequent, and then stopped altogether.

And that, more or less, is everything I knew about Anne and Jonah Boyd, until the day several decades later when, rather out of the blue, Ben Wright called me up to tell me that he was in town, and that he wanted to invite me to dinner.

This was not something I expected. Although Ben and I had remained on civil terms through the years, we had never become what you would call "friends." Indeed, since Nancy's death, I'd seen him exactly once, when he'd given a reading at a Wellspring bookstore: The line for autographs had been so long, I hadn't bothered to wait. Still, I'd followed the trajectory of his career with interest and some vicarious pride. It was a strange story, as likely to inspire cynicism as hope, depending on your point of view and time of life. At some point after Jonah Boyd's visit, Ben had stopped writing poems and started writing stories, which he proceeded to send off to *The New Yorker* with an alacrity to match that of his poetry days. Like the poems, the stories came back unfailingly with rejection forms attached, provoking despondency in Ben and a sort of futile fist-shaking at the universe in Nancy. Still, he kept sending new ones. He was by now a junior in high school, and though he remained an indifferent student, nonetheless I think he took it for granted that he would get into Wellspring, as his more academically minded brother and sister had before him. And in this delusory belief, Nancy, out of the same misplaced impulse that had led her to give him false hope about his writing, backed him up. I shall never forget the black April morning when the rejection letter came—Nancy trying to console him, saying, "It doesn't matter. Who needs a big-name college? You're too good for them." To which Ben replied, "But you were the one who told me I'd get in! You said it was a sure thing! You promised me!" Round and round they went, her efforts to persuade him that the rejection was not a tragedy only fortifying his conviction that it was. A tragedy, moreover, for which she bore ultimate responsibility: Because she had encouraged him, she was easier to blame than that pitiless abstraction, the university.

Ben went off to college: not to Harvard or Yale (they also turned him down) but to Bradford, where Ernest still had connections in the admissions office. He majored in European history. As in high school, he was an indifferent student. He continued to write, publishing a few stories in undergraduate magazines, and even winning the recently endowed Jonah Boyd Prize for Short Fiction, which brought with it a hundred-dollar gift certificate at the campus bookstore. (Nancy kept note of these achievements in a discreet brown leather scrap-book, which took pride of place on the piano.) Then after graduation he moved to New York City, hoping, like a character in a Willa Cather story, to make a name for himself there before returning triumphant to the home town that had failed to appreciate him. (That Wellspring, with its symphony orchestra and coffee bars, bore not the slightest resemblance to Cather's windswept Nebraska hamlets seems not to have deterred him in the least in this ambition: further proof of Ernest's theory that his son lived half in a dream world.) I think he was imagining ticker-tape parades, and speeches during which the university president would hit himself on the head for having undervalued Ben, all the while marveling at the grace, the utter lack of vainglory, that marked his heroic return. The dolts who had bullied him in high school would stare up dumbfounded, his former teachers would claim to have encouraged him when they had not . . . And through it all he would just smile and wave, the very embodiment of generosity, a man so successful he could afford to forgive. Let's not mince words. Ben, at this stage, had delusions of grandeur. He was avid to explore New York—but *his* New York, which was the New York of *New Yorker* covers, foggy and wistful and consisting exclusively of capacious apartments in which well-dressed women drank whole-leaf tea and talked about Tolstoy. The bohemian East Village to which his coevals were flocking held no allure for him. He was too much of a snob for railroad flats. Rather than move in with downtown friends, he sublet a noisy efficiency apartment above a vegetable market on Second Avenue—overpriced, but it *was* East Seventy-fourth Street. To survive, he took a job shelving at the Strand; still, his mother had to send him money each month, sometimes surreptitiously, as Ernest did not approve of their supporting an adult son in this way. The several girlfriends he went through shared his father's uneasiness—especially once Ben finished his novel, and was unable to publish it, and set to work on a second novel, and couldn't publish that one, either. As he told me later, he was too arrogant to condescend to getting a full-time job. "Really, I was a little shit," he said, smiling at his own callowness as one can only from the vantage point of great success achieved later in life. And when, eventually, he did move back to Wellspring, it was neither in triumph nor by choice. For Ernest had one afternoon been murdered in his office, and Nancy had been diagnosed with an inoperable brain tumor, and keeping the house on Florizona Avenue for her children was now the driving ambition of her remaining days. She more or less insisted that Ben come home to help her in her campaign, and he came not unwillingly, for as he explained to me, it was a relief to have an excuse to get out of New York, a city which, because it had once been the locus of his hope, was with each day that passed becoming more and more the nexus of his despair. A third novel had now gone untaken. He could no longer abide having to watch, he said, the spectacle of writers younger than himself achieving the very goal—publication—that eluded him. And he was no longer so young himself. He was nearly thirty. The girl he claimed to love was growing exasperated with his indolence, eager to marry him yet wary of taking on the financial burden of an unemployed (and possibly unemployable) husband. Perhaps if he could offer her a house, he reasoned, he might be able to convince her not to look for someone else.

It was at this point that he reentered my orbit. Except for Daphne and Glenn's wedding and the occasional Thanksgiving (he did not always come home, often preferring to be a "stray" at the apartment of some New York friend), it had really been quite a few years since I'd spent a sustained chunk of time in his company. And now here he stood on Nancy's doorstep, a young man. His long hair fell to form a sort of awning over his forehead. His nose reminded me of his father's. All told, he looked alarmingly like his father.

Since Ernest's murder, I had been promoted; I was now office manager for the entire psych department, a job that kept me on my toes all week and some weekends. I no longer lived in Eaton Manor, but rented a house of my own, far from the noise of the freeway, and had several lovers, one of whom wanted to leave his wife for me. My life was busy. Even so, I tried to spend as much time as I could with Nancy. It was my fervent hope that the Wrights would succeed in keeping their house, which I, too, simply could not imagine in other hands. Nancy was by now very sick, as much from the radiation and chemotherapy courses she was undergoing as from the tumor itself, though to their credit, Ben and Daphne did everything they could to keep her out of the hospital. She dreaded the hospital, and feared especially the prospect of dying there.

Although he visited only twice in that period, Mark sent flowers almost daily. He was recently married to a Canadian girl, a lawyer with much disposable income, his house in the Toronto suburbs (of which Nancy showed me pictures) so lavishly bourgeois that I could only think what an odd destination it was for him, given that he had begun his journey in a Datsun with no reverse gear. During his visits, Mark stayed at the Ritz-Carlton; in the afternoons he would stop by to interrogate the nurse who made periodic visits, or scrutinize insurance statements in search of small errors on the basis of which he could chastise Ben or Daphne. This atmosphere in which a dying and increasingly demented woman lay propped up in her bed, smelling of roses and disinfectant, her bald head wrapped in a turban that made her look like some sort of antique film actress, must have seemed more than a little bizarre to Daphne's children, though they were still young at the time, and reeling from the suddenness with which their mother had left their father. I spent a lot of hours at Nancy's bedside, for she always recognized faces, even if, toward the end, she hardly seemed to know where she was. Where the IV needle entered her hand, she said that a tulip bulb was sprouting. She thought she was a flower bed. One afternoon she confided that a mule got into her bed with her every night. "But he's a very polite mule," she added. "He never moves or makes noise."

On another occasion she spoke of Jonah Boyd. "Did he ever find that novel?" she asked.

"No, he didn't," I said.

"Tell him to look in the pantry. You know there was some foie gras Ernest brought back from Paris—a tin of foie gras— and for months, for the life of me, I couldn't find it. But then it turned up way at the back of the pantry, behind the soup cans."

"But Nancy," I said, "Jonah Boyd is dead. He died years ago, in a car crash."

"Anne should never have married him. Clifford was a decent man. Boring, but decent. But she wanted adventure, and I suppose she got it."

"Yes."

"She comes over every Saturday. We play four-hand piano."

"No, Nancy. _I_ come over every Saturday. We play four-hand piano."

"Next week we're trying the Grand Duo."

"Do you think you're up for it?"

"Well, you know what my husband says. You never can tell till you try."

Ernest had never once in his life said anything so optimistic.

"No, you never can," I agreed. I suppose it was as good a principle to follow as any.

After Nancy's death, I lost touch with Ben once more. With his third of the money from the sale of the house, he moved to Milwaukee, and bought a small house of his own. Milwaukee was where the girlfriend came from. Her name was Molly. They got married, and, so far as I knew, he returned to writing.

By way of an inheritance from Nancy, I received all of her music and the scrapbook in which she kept the stories Ben had published. I think she must have figured that I could be counted on to keep up the scrapbook, and so when Ben at long last did publish a novel, about four years after her death, out of a sense of duty, I kept my eyes peeled for mentions of him in newspapers and magazines. As it happened, there were none that I could find. The novel, which was called *The Sky,* got very little attention, and went quickly out of print. Later, Ben renounced it. And yet with his next novel, *Backwards,* he won for himself not only accolades from critics and an important prize, but a youthful following that remained devoted to him until his death, buying his books as soon as they appeared and filling the lecture halls and bookstores in which he gave readings. This second published novel of Ben's was a road novel, and its subject, not surprisingly, was the fate of the draft dodgers; as it opens, the sixteen-year-old narrator is on his way to Vancouver in a Toyota with no reverse gear, intent on finding and moving in with his brother. *Backwards* was optioned for a film and sat for about six weeks near the bottom of the *New York Times* best-seller list. Each Sunday I dutifully scissored the list out of the newspaper and pasted it into Nancy's scrapbook, which was now running out of pages.

I would have to buy another one, I realized, preferably covered in the same restrained brown leather—yet I could find nothing even remotely like it anywhere in Wellspring. Or Pasadena. Sifting through the supply of blank scrapbooks at Vroman's one Saturday, I found myself wondering what had become of the little shop in Verona where Jonah Boyd had bought *his* notebooks. Was it still in business? Were the notebooks even made anymore? Of course, in trying to envision the shop, I had only his description to go on; even if I did make it to Verona someday, even if the shop still existed, the likelihood of my nosing it out was slim. That Thanksgiving, Ernest had asked Boyd what he would do if his notebooks ever ceased to be manufactured, and Boyd had barely been able to answer (not that this mattered very much, in the end). It seemed to me, that day at Vroman's, that Ernest had been wise to decry such a mystic dependency on things and houses as both Boyd and Nancy were susceptible to, and in silent support of him, I picked out the scrapbook that was the least like Nancy's I could find—indeed, the one most likely to offend her sensibilities, all hot pink and yellow daisies, with a huge Hello Kitty rising up in the background like some grotesque parade float. In this, I continued the record of her son's career.

It was now 1997. Ben was no longer living in Milwaukee. He had divorced Molly, and taken a job teaching in the Creative Writing program at the University of Maryland. He had remarried—Amy, also a writer. Another book appeared, not a novel this time, but a memoir of his California childhood, *The Eucalyptus*, which of course I read with avidity, since it was also, in some sense, the story of my life. I must admit, Ben's descriptive prowess impressed me. He captured vividly the flavor of that house on Florizona Avenue, devoting particular attention to the

Thanksgivings, and interweaving into his story that of Phil, the least noticeable of the strays, who one spring afternoon, his Ph.D. thesis having just been rejected for the fourth time, knocked on the door of Ernest's office, and when Ernest opened it, shot him in the face. He would have shot Glenn, too, but Glenn happened to be in the bathroom. Ernest died before he could say a word. In the memoir, Ben writes at length of the yellow tape sealing off the crime scene, not to mention the phalanx of news reporters and squad cars that surrounded his parents' house, and that seemed so out of place on Florizona Avenue. All of this I, too, remembered. I was there, in the office, when Ernest died. I held him as he died. And then afterward, without saying anything of my own grief, I held Nancy while she wept in disbelief at the idea that for so many Thanksgivings she had nursed a viper at her table. And all that time Phil had seemed so benign—so boring, even—that skinny boy with his big appetite! Curiously, this discordance between appearance and reality seemed to preoccupy her much more than the fact that her husband had been murdered. Might there have been warning signs? A picture of Daphne had disappeared one Thanksgiving from the mantel; someone had left some poisoned meat in the backyard that Little Hans had eaten. (He'd survived.) Now she wondered if Jonah Boyd's notebooks had really been lost, or if perhaps Phil, for mysterious reasons of his own, had stolen them. "If only we'd seen," Nancy lamented. "If only we'd noticed."

I tried to remind her that Ernest himself had liked and trusted Phil. Given that *he* had harbored no suspicions, there was no reason for Nancy to beat herself up now. "I just wonder," she answered. But soon enough the brain tumor put an end even to wondering.

Both the local and the national media pounced on the story

of Ernest's murder. Glenn was interviewed by Dan Rather—not just because he was Ernest's protégé and Phil's nemesis but as an authority on psychosis. His diagnosis was that under the pressure of seeing his career about to collapse, and after so many years of watching his contemporaries move ahead of him, Phil had just snapped. "There is in all of us," Glenn told Dan Rather, "the potential to do something unspeakable. What fascinates psychologists is the question of what restrains some, while others are suddenly propelled to make fateful decisions."

All of this is in Ben's memoir, and much more—the "real" story behind Mark's flight to Canada (as opposed to Ben's fictional account), and the struggle to keep the house, and Daphne's divorce, and Nancy's death—and yet, curiously, there is not a single mention of Jonah or Anne Boyd, and less curiously, no mention of me. I do not appear even once. I am left out wholesale. Later I asked him why this was. "Oh, Denny," he said, "writers always have to make choices. You can't put everything in a book. Besides, you were never really *involved* in any of it, were you? You were just—I don't know—there. On the sidelines."

The memoir, for Ben, was the biggest success of all. He went on talk shows. To promote the book, which had been trans-lated into something like twenty languages, he made a Eur-opean tour. Back in College Park, he threatened to quit his job at the university, and in exchange for a promise to stay on, he got a reduction of his teaching load along with a substantial pay raise. Amy, unhappy that her career was not matching his, left him for a heart surgeon. Seeing no reason to stay in Maryland, now that his ex-wife was living down the street in a much grander style than he could afford, Ben put out the word that he would entertain offers from other schools, on the condition that they be willing to pay him twice what he was earning at Maryland in exchange for only one semester of teaching a year. And he could get away with that. He had become famous enough that he could write his own ticket.

It was then, to his own amazement, that he got the letter from the provost at Wellspring—the same provost to whom Nancy had made her appeal, not so long before, to keep the house, and who had rebuffed her. It seemed that a rich alumnus, a dabbler in fiction himself, had of late given the university a substantial sum of money for the purpose of endowing a chair for a writer-in-residence: For this position, Ben was now quietly encouraged to apply. He did so eagerly. A few weeks later, in Wellspring to be interviewed, he telephoned me. As it happened, I had taken early retirement a year earlier. I now owned my own house—a two-bedroom, concrete-block affair in a modest neighborhood of Springwell. The last thing I expected in those unbusy days was for Ben Wright to call, and not only to call, but to invite me to dinner.

We met at the faculty club. Amazingly, even though I had worked at the university for more than thirty years, and knew its ins and outs better than anyone alive, until that evening I had never once been to the faculty club, the scene of Nancy's raging at poor Bess Dalrymple. Ernest had disdained the place as stuffy, and after he had been killed . . . well, who else but her boss would invite a secretary to eat dinner in a gloomy, formal room where the food was expensive and bad? For my retirement party, I'd had the choice of the faculty club or a restaurant, and had opted for a rather festive Mexican place, with sangria and flirty waiters. La Piñata was more my speed, just as a nice, comfortable denim skirt with an elastic waistband was more my style . . . And now here I sat, waiting for Ben in a dining room hushed by heavy draperies that smelled of boiled cabbage, while around me faculty widows I recognized from Nancy's long-ago tea parties sipped white wine and gossiped in low voices. The suit I wore was as uncomfortable as the one I'd put on decades before, that first Thanksgiving I'd spent with the Wrights.

After a while Ben came in. He now had the belly that comes after forty, and a heavy beard, white speckling the brown. Still, I had no trouble recognizing him. "Denny, what a pleasure," he said, and kissed me on the cheek.

"You look so much like your father I almost fell out of my chair," I said.

"So I've been told about fifty times today."

He sat down. A waiter approached, a man older than me, whom I recognized from the staff parking lot. Ben demanded wine, and the waiter withdrew. "Listen, I have some news," he said. "It's not official yet, so you'll have to keep this to yourself for the time being. They've offered me the job. Writer-in-residence in the English department, one semester a year."

"Wow," I said. "Congratulations."

The waiter brought the wine, as well as menus. "Kind of incredible, isn't it, when you consider that back in the dark ages, the damn place didn't even see fit to admit me? But that's neither here nor there. The point is, now that I've got the job, I can buy it back."

"Buy what back?"

He looked at me as if I were an idiot. "The house, of course."

"Oh, the house," I said; and then, as my train of thought caught up with his: "You mean your parents' house?"

121

"What other house would I be talking about?" he asked, laughing. And he was right to laugh: Clearly I *was* an idiot to have imagined that just because, over the years, I had more or less stopped thinking about the house, he would have also.

"But is it even on the market? I remember Nancy sold it to a couple of law professors."

"Yes, Travis and Eleanor Ault. But then they split up and sold it to a Dr. Clark from the medical school. He kept it a few years, made some horrible quote-unquote *improvements* in the garden—they tore out the old fish pond, can you believe it?—and then *he* sold it to the people who own it now. Their name is Shoemaker. She's in zoology and he's some sort of higher-up on the development council. Anyway, it's not for sale, at least officially, but when I went in for my interview with the provost, he basically said, 'What can we do to get you to come?' So I mentioned the house, and he made a few phone calls, and the long and the short of it is, they're willing to sell if the price is right. They're asking a lot—close to two million— much more than the appraised value, so I'll probably have to do a deal on my new book before I write it, just to have the cash for the down payment. And to think that my father paid thirty thousand dollars for that place, and now it's worth . . . But there's no point in going into the numbers. Wellspring owes this to me, after what they did to my mother. Of course I'll have to take out a huge mortgage. Luckily I can manage it. Barely. Thank God I don't have kids!"

"Congratulations," I repeated—rather weakly, for the figure of two million dollars had left me dumbfounded.

"I'm glad you're happy," Ben said, even though I had said nothing to suggest that I was. "You see, I was thinking it all over this afternoon, in my room over at the Ritz-Carlton, and I realized that you were the only person around who would understand why this mattered so much to me. I haven't told my sister yet. I've been putting it off. I suppose I'm frightened how she'll react."

"Why?"

"Well, we never talked about it then—it was too important to present a united front—but when we were trying to persuade the provost to let us keep the place, in the back of both our minds, and my mother's, too, I suppose, there was always this lingering question: In the event that we won, which of us would actually live there? We could hardly have shared the house. We would have driven each other crazy. And of course Mark would have insisted that we buy him out of his share, and then would the one who did stay have to buy out the other one? At that stage, neither of us could have afforded to. I know Daphne would have tried to trump me with her kids—you know, I have children, and you don't, and therefore I need the house more than you do, so the kids can trample the flowers and clog up the pool with their toys."

"But why should any of it matter now? Daphne doesn't even live in Wellspring anymore. She lives in Portland. She has a house of her own."

"My feelings exactly. Nor should we allow ourselves to forget that *she's* not the one who's just been offered a plum position thanks to a reputation she worked very hard and many years to attain. She tried to get a job herself here, remember, and failed. Still, I'd be foolish to assume she'll react rationally. These things are so personal. And anyway, she never understood my mother's spiritual attachment to that house. For her it was just plain greed. She wanted all the space. She wanted the pool."

"Well, maybe if you approach her in the right way, she'll come around," I said—lame, but as a response, it seemed close to the probable truth.

Ben lifted his glass. "Let's have a toast. To 302 Florizona Avenue."

"*Cin-cin,*" I said.

"That's funny. *Cin-cin* was how my father always toasted. I wonder what he'd think of all this—how things have turned out. He never had much faith in me."

"That's not true."

"Oh come on, Denny, you know it as well as I do. He pretty much wrote me off as a loser from the get-go. Wouldn't he be surprised to see where I've landed? A higher salary than *he* ever pulled in." He was gazing at his wine as he said this, his expression more introspective than gloating. "You know, I don't usually think of myself as a religious person, or even a particularly spiritual person, but when you look at how things have turned out—well, how can you help but wonder if it wasn't all meant to be?"

"In what sense?"

"I mean, consider the coincidences. The very year I decide to look for a new job, Wellspring endows a position for a writer-in-residence. Fifty people must have applied, yet they choose me. I ask about the house, figuring there isn't a chance in hell it'll be on the market, and the Shoemakers say they'll sell. So now, by getting the house back, I've fulfilled my mother's fondest wish. By getting the job, I've fulfilled my own. When things work out like that, it's hard not to think that there's a pattern, or a purpose, or that you've got a guardian angel. Although God knows if I do, he fell down on the job. For years."

124

"Well, but you're discounting your own books. They're what got you the job. Oh, and by the way, I'm afraid I haven't read the novels, only the memoir, which I liked very much."

"Don't even bother with the first one. The first one is pathetic. Since my stuff started selling, my publishers have been trying to convince me to let them bring it out in paperback, but I won't allow it."

Our food arrived—a depressing vignette of salmon filets and heartless little vegetables, two carrots, three potato balls, a sprig of parsley: the sort of meal after which you have to go out and get yourself a cheeseburger. I took an unencouraging bite (the salmon was dry); thought suddenly of Jonah Boyd, that last dinner I'd eaten with him and Anne and Ben at the Pie 'n Burger. Odd that in all the years since, Ben and I had never talked about that Thanksgiving. And now, as if he were reading my mind, he suddenly said, "Remember the Thanksgiving when the Boyds came?"

"Funny, I just was."

"Very strange, what happened."

"It still surprises me that the notebooks never turned up. You'd think that eventually someone would have—"

"Well, but Denny, you don't really believe they were lost, do you? You know what my mother thought."

"What—that Phil stole them?"

"It would make sense. He did a lot of creepy things hounding girls in the psych department, stealing things. He hated my father, he hated Glenn. I wouldn't put it past him."

"But what would the notebooks have to do with any of that?"

"Who knows? Who can penetrate a psychotic mind? Maybe he was jealous because Dad and Glenn were paying so much attention to Jonah Boyd that night. And of course, we'll never find out, will we, because even if we asked him, Phil wouldn't tell us. Not where he is." Ben drank more wine. "And to think that all those years he came to Thanksgiving, and nobody ever guessed . . . You know, since then I've read both Boyd's novels, and I've got to tell you, I really don't see what the big deal was. Does that sound callous? I guess what I mean is that he was one of those writers who looked, in his time, as if he was going to be important, but who if he had lived . . . well, he probably would have ended up right where he is now. Out of print. I hate to sound so brutal, but it's true. It's a theory of mine that the destinations we're supposed to get to—in art, life, relationships—they're set in advance. It's just that there are shorter routes and longer routes. Like in novels. In novels I can accept coincidences if the objective is to move the story faster to where it would have gone anyway. It drives me crazy when the only reason for the coincidence is to alter everything, blow the characters' lives to smithereens."

"But isn't that what happened to Boyd, when his notebooks were stolen? His life blown to smithereens?"

"No, that's my point! It only *looked* that way. In a cosmic sense, I'm truly convinced, the end would have been the same."

"Maybe for his books. But he might not have died."

The waiter took our plates away. I had hardly touched my salmon, eaten only one of the potato balls. Nor did it seem worth the trouble to order dessert. Ben paid our bill, and we went out to the parking lot, where once again he exhorted me not to read his first novel: "*Backwards,* yes. It's good. But the first one—embarrassing. An apprentice effort. If I could vaporize every copy, I would."

Why should a writer be so determined to suppress his own book? Perhaps Ben feared that if this fledgling novel were brought back into print, its very badness would cause readers to reassess the later, more popular works . . . In any case, I promised not to read *The Sky*. He drove off in his rental car, his destination the Ritz-Carlton, while I drove off in my Dodge Dart, my destination the Pie 'n Burger. I sat at the counter and wondered where it came from, Ben's impulse to attribute chance events to mystic intervention; certainly not from Ernest. It was more like Nancy to see patterns and plans everywhere, or think in terms of fixed destinations. After all, believing that a house can be more than an assemblage of bricks and cement and shingles is not so different from believing in a guardian angel, and if Ben did have a protector, no doubt that spirit was incarnate in 302 Florizona Avenue. As for me, I harbored no such illusions—but then again, I hadn't grown up in that house. The sense of birthright in which Ben, despite everything he'd endured, continued to have faith—I'd never known it.

The necessary cheeseburger arrived. I took a bite. And now, as if to illustrate the very matters Ben had spoken of, the waiter who had served us at the faculty club stepped through the door to the Pie 'n Burger and took the stool next to mine. We nodded at each other. He ordered a slice of banana cream pie, opened a copy of *Field and Stream*. So perhaps this was serendipity, and the waiter and I were destined to fall in love. Or perhaps this was misfortune, and when I finished my cheeseburger, he would follow me out to the parking lot and strangle me. Or perhaps nothing would happen—coincidence within which no pattern could be discerned. The last of these hypotheses turned out to be correct. We did not speak, and after I paid my bill, I drove home without incident.

On the way, I took Florizona Avenue. It had been years since I'd had occasion to cruise that memorable thoroughfare. Passing 302, I noticed that the Shoemakers had lined the path that led from the street to the front door with Malibu lights. Even in the dark you could see what a lovely house it was— harmonious in its proportions, not grand exactly, but not cozy, either—a house that encouraged you to lead a life of large gestures, to leap about and sing and flex your muscles. And soon it would be Ben's. Now that I thought about it, his luck really was extraordinary. Yes, he would have his sister to contend with, as well as the anxiety that accompanies any hefty financial burden. And yet, my hunch was that, despite these troubles, he would be happy. Grief and frustration and loss would leave no indelible marks upon him, and this was good, for a kind of unalloyed happiness has to exist some-where, a sort of floor model of happiness, if we are to go on thinking that such a thing is worth hoping for.

Needless to say, when I got home that night, my own little house seemed flimsy and trivial. I could not sleep for the traffic noise, the glare of the streetlamp through sheer curtains. And then in the morning, the prospect of another day without work—another day to try to fill up with activity, now that I was retired—depressed me, and made me eager for a project. Already I had reorganized the pantry and cleaned out my file cabinet. Now I set to work alphabetizing the books. I started with Jane Austen, and after a few hours arrived at *W,* Benjamin Wright coming just before Ernest. Of course I only had the second two of Ben's, *Backwards* and *The Eucalyptus.* And really, his adamance that I not read that first novel *was*

128

peculiar; could it really be as bad as all that? Despite my promise, I was curious to see what the fuss was about. So I got in the car and drove to campus, to the library; I looked up *The Sky* on the computer, wrote down the call number, and rode the elevator to the fourth floor of the stacks: twentieth-century American fiction. But the book wasn't there. Downstairs, I asked a librarian. She looked on her screen. "It's missing," she said with a frown. "Very strange. Not checked out, just . . . missing. You might try the municipal library."

I did as she suggested. At the municipal library, once again, I looked up *The Sky;* located the right shelf. And once again, the book wasn't there. "It disappeared months ago," the municipal librarian told me. "Happens sometimes. People pry off the security tags. Or some weirdo who doesn't like the writer tears it up and flushes it down the toilet. The plumbing disasters we've had!"

Now this was *really* strange. Why should *two* copies have gone missing? The novel was indeed out of print—a phone call to Vroman's verified that—so I drove to Bartram's, Wellspring's premier used bookstore, and asked after it. The clerk laughed in my face. "It's the rarest of the rare!" he said, and recommended that I try Booksource, in Pasadena, the owner of which became briefly animated when I mentioned the title only, it turned out, because she hoped I had one to sell. "I've got a list of ten people waiting to grab up a copy as soon as one comes in," she said.

"Really? Is it that hard to come by?"

"He's very popular. And everyone wants the complete works. By the way, have you heard the rumor that he's coming to teach at Wellspring?"

"Anywhere else I might try?"

"The Library of Congress."

"Very funny," I said, and left.

As you have probably already determined, I am not a woman who backs away from a challenge. Indeed, the bookstore owner's insistence that I would never find a copy of *The Sky* now fortified my determination to do so. And so that afternoon I got out the Los Angeles County Yellow Pages and called used bookstores in Glendale, Los Feliz, Hollywood, North Hollywood, Arcadia, Santa Monica, Venice, and Long Beach. Nothing. I called Van Nuys, Ventura, Brentwood, and Beverly Hills. Still nothing. Unfazed, I went farther afield. I called San Francisco, Seattle. I called Powell's in Portland. I called Denver. Finally I called the Strand in New York, where Ben had once worked, and there, at last, I hit pay dirt: a copy had just come in, first edition with dust jacket. Slightly foxed. Two hundred dollars. I bought it on the spot and arranged to have it sent.

The book arrived five days later. Rather impatiently, I pulled it from its envelope. (What was "foxing," anyway?) The cover image struck me as curious: a zipper bisecting a serene cloud, revealing blackness and rain underneath. And how youthful Ben's face looked, gazing out at me from the back of the jacket, his hair parted in the middle in imitation of his brother! I read the dedication—"For my mother"—thought of Nancy, then turned to the first page.

"To make love in a balloon . . ."

My neck jerked upward; there was no mistaking the cracked baritone voice that uttered these words—the voice in my head—though it had been almost thirty years since I'd heard it.

Ten

LITERATURE HAS FOR too long ignored the perspective of the secretary. Overworked and underpaid, never given anything close to adequate credit for her labors (for example, as I said earlier, *I* wrote most of Ernest's books), praised—when she is praised—only for such stalwart attributes as efficiency, reliability, and maternal understanding, she goes through her career generally unthanked except in a photocopying crisis, very occasionally mentioned in the fourth paragraph of a long acknowledgments page, never the object of a book dedication, never named in the memoirs, never left anything in the will. Do not assume, though, that just because she is invisible, she is anyone's fool. On the contrary, either because her employer confides in her, or because she is his mistress, or because, as part of her daily routine, she books his plane tickets and files his credit card bills and takes his messages, she often ends up knowing more about him than anyone else does, even his wife. Even the word secretary contains a secret. Trustworthiness is her watchword. Still, there is in her one allegiance that supersedes even that which she pledges, implicitly, to her boss, and for the sake of which, if necessary, she would betray him. And that is her allegiance to other secretaries.

After I read *The Sky,* I didn't know what to do. My first thought was that Ben must have stolen Jonah Boyd's notebooks, finished the novel they contained, and published it as his own. Yet how could I be sure of this? Three decades had passed since that Thanksgiving, and my memory of Boyd's reading was hazy. It was equally possible that Ben had stolen only the first chapter of the novel—the only part with which I was familiar—or that he had stolen just the idea, the germ of *Gonesse,* and the first line. But if that were the case, wouldn't *someone* have noticed? Boyd must have read aloud from the manuscript to others besides us. And Anne certainly would have seen—assuming Anne was still alive. A quick call to directory assistance in Bradford yielded no listing under her name. What was her maiden name, then? Or had she remarried?

We secretaries can always recognize each other, even over the phone. Something in the lilt of the "hello," a certain crispness of tone when picking up . . . I heard it immediately in the voice of Marjorie Armstrong, Clifford Armstrong's second wife, when I called to ask if he might have any information as to his first wife's whereabouts. "Armstrong residence," she said, and somehow at that moment I knew not only that she had once been a secretary, but that she had been *his* secretary, and that he had married her after Anne had left him.

That morning Marjorie and I talked for more than an hour. As soon as she realized that I, too, was a secretary, she dropped her veneer of implacability and became intimate, confiding. She told me that Clifford had Parkinson's disease, and could no longer speak. She told me that of course she remembered Anne, and had even liked her, sort of—Anne, whose tie-dyed skirts and hennaed hair had implied possibilities of liberation never before considered by the women of Bradford. She told me that the coffin factory had of late been made over into a sort of arts and crafts mall with a café where you could get the best pecan chicken salad. In fact, the only thing she didn't tell me—because she couldn't—was what had become of Anne. Although she recalled that after Boyd's death, Anne had remarried—an engineering professor, Marjorie thought—beyond that, the trail went cold. She'd stopped seeing Anne in the supermarket. She'd stopped thinking about Anne, who was, after all, not a secretary.

It didn't matter. I was on the scent. Marjorie gave me the number of her friend Pat, who, like me, was retired, but had for many years been secretary to the chair of Bradford's engineering department. I called Pat, and she told me that she, too, remembered Anne, who had married Bruce Ridge, an expert in highway cloverleaf design. A few years after the marriage, Bruce had been wooed away from Bradford with an offer to be chair of the engineering department at the University of Kansas. At Kansas, I spoke to Loretta, who said that yes, the Ridges had lived in Lawrence in the mid-eighties, but that after a few years the midwestern winters had gotten to be too much for them. So Bruce had taken early retirement, and they'd moved to Florida. Tarpon Springs. This was in 1989. Loretta gave me a number in Tarpon Springs, which I called. A woman answered.

"May I speak to Anne Ridge?" I asked.

"What's this in reference to?" the woman said.

A secretary.

"I'm sorry to bother you," I said, "but I'm trying to locate some information about Anne Ridge, formerly Anne Boyd. The widow of the novelist Jonah Boyd."

"Jonah Boyd!"

"Do you know him?"

"I should say I know him," the woman said. "I'm his daughter."

Her name—Jonah Boyd's eldest daughter's name—is Susan. She is now forty-eight years old, and lives in Tampa, where she works as a legal secretary. Long divorced; the mother of two teenage daughters. From her, I learned much more about Jonah Boyd, and about Anne.

Biography is a funny thing. Why some people get them and others don't is beyond me. For instance, as I write this, two academics—two!—are preparing biographies of Ernest. (Why either thinks anyone is going to shell out thirty-five bucks for the life of an obscure Freudian is beyond me.) And yet there is no biography, and never has been, and probably never will be, of Jonah Boyd. Even on the Internet, only a few mentions of him come up, mostly paraphrases from an old entry in *Contemporary Authors*. The abyss of obscurity into which he has fallen is so deep that even the spindly arm of biography will not reach there: evidence, perhaps, that Ben's assessment of his work was correct.

I have managed, in the intervening years, to learn more about him. He was born in 1924 in Abilene, Texas. He was the middle of three sons. In Abilene, he married his childhood sweetheart, Mary Burrows, straight out of high school. She was pregnant, as it happens, and gave birth to Susan on her nineteenth birthday. A few years later she had Bradley, and then Karen. Mary worked in a supermarket while Jonah went to college—Texas Tech. He did not graduate. The Korean War interrupted his studies. After he got back, he started writing, and was bold in his ambitions: Like Ben, he sent his stories only to the most prestigious magazines, to *The New Yorker* and *Esquire* and *The Paris Review*. Unlike Ben, he received encouraging replies. His career only really got started, though, when he attended a sort of literary conference in Dallas at which he met a famous New York editor, like him a drunk. They went out drinking together, and at the end of the evening, the editor offered Boyd a contract for a novel on the basis of a single sentence. (Susan can't remember what the sentence was, only that it never made it into the final draft.) Boyd feared that when he got back to New York, the editor would renege on his drunken promise, but he didn't, and a contract came through. In due course the novel, *Dog Bone Soup,* was published. This was in 1959.

Dog Bone Soup is based on Boyd's experiences in Korea. It is a hard, grotesque, funny book, and it gained Boyd a modicum of admiration, if little money. To earn his keep, he was teaching composition at a junior college in Dallas. Mary had gone to work for the company that published the yellow pages. Both drank. Boyd slept in the afternoons, and stayed up until dawn writing. The novel on which he was at work was the one that he would later describe to Anne as having "gone down like a lead balloon." It was titled *The World in Miniature,* and it took place in England and Italy during the Great War, but I can assure you that, contrary to what Boyd himself believed, it is not by any stretch of the imagination a "lead balloon." Yes, it is long and arcane and in some parts boring (this is probably why it wasn't very successful); yes, in its juxtaposition of bloody battle scenes and moments of romantic proto-homosexual pathos, its weird tonal hybridizing of Louis L'Amour and Somerset Maugham, it jars the ear and the mind; yet for me it succeeds—mostly, I think, because this strange admixture of Texas swagger and bookish refinement embodies perfectly the spirit of Jonah Boyd, as I briefly knew him. He was a paradox in many ways. Thus Susan remembers that even though he often drank until he vomited in the kitchen sink, and beat his wife, he was always immensely careful with his mustache, which he modeled on Proust's own. She recalls him letting her hold his mustache brush, run the bristles through the thicket of hair.

After *The World in Miniature,* Boyd went through a period of severe writer's block, one that his drinking and the four/four teaching load imposed on him by the junior college only worsened. He managed to get himself together enough to apply for some grants, though, and in the spring of 1967, much to his surprise, he won a Guggenheim fellowship—enough money to allow him, at last, to take a leave of absence from his job, and travel, for one blessed spring, in Europe. This was the trip during which he happened upon the leather and paper goods shop in Verona where he found the notebooks. As he told Susan in a letter, he had just arrived in Verona, it was late afternoon, and he had left the legal pad he was carrying with him on the train (a foretaste of future absentmindedness). In a bit of stupor he'd wandered into the shop, and been captivated both by its owner and her merchandise. Even today Susan can quote much of that letter from memory, especially the part about the white gloves.

In April, he returned to Dallas. It was a painful reentry. After Provence and Venice and Rome, Texas seemed to him cheesy and insular. Having gotten habituated to eating tartares and salads with *gesiers,* he could no longer bear the food Mary cooked him. When she served him a TV dinner, he threw it at the TV. Nor could he bear his job, the bored students in whom it was his thankless task to instill some respect for literature. One evening at a party he picked a fight with the chairman of his department, and bloodied his nose. He was fired after that. You might think the nose incident would have spelled the end of Boyd's academic career, but in fact, in literary circles, it rather enhanced his reputation; after all, this was the age when Norman Mailer was lionized for trying to kill his wife. And so when the chance to teach at Bradford arose—brokered by a mutual friend, another drunken novelist whose brother happened to be the chairman of the Bradford English department—he jumped at it as a sort of lifeline. Not that Bradford was any paradise—it was merely an industrial New England town in which most of the factories were closed—but at least it was *east,* and, as such, in the same general direction as Europe. Boyd didn't even tell his family where he was going; he just packed a suitcase, kissed them good-bye, and drove off, promising to call in a few days. That was the last Susan ever saw of him, because when he finally did call—six months later—it was to tell Mary that he would not contest a divorce. She could keep the shitty house and the crappy car. He felt bad for the children, but could see no way at this point to be of any use to them; once he finished his new novel, and got rich, he would try to make up to them for his cruelty, at least by sending some cash.

It goes without saying that at this stage Susan Boyd's feelings toward her father were ambivalent, to say the least. On the one hand, his departure wrecked her chances of going to college, as now she had to take care of her brother and sister. On the other hand, she understood his reasons for leaving: "Because it was a dead end, that household," she told me, "and there was no way, given the environment, that he could have ever finished another book. In retrospect, it's amazing that he managed to get out the books that he did." Although, during his Bradford years, Boyd wrote his daughter a score of letters, and called her at least once a week, whenever she hazarded the possibility of a visit, he found an excuse to put her off. Later, when she learned about the lost notebooks and his resulting relapse into alcoholism, she thought she understood at last what had lain behind this seemingly inexplicable standoffishness. And yet at the time his refusal to see her provoked in her only perplexity and hurt—"as if somehow he was ashamed of us, or embarrassed by us, me and Karen and Bradley. Of course, he wouldn't tell me what was really going on. I guess he couldn't bear to."

Susan met Anne the winter that Boyd died, when she flew to Bradford, with her siblings, for his funeral. Bradley—now a baker in Houston—was chiefly interested in smoking pot, while Karen put most of her energy into the small stakes beauty pageants that she habitually entered but never won because she was fat. Their mother had gone beyond the pale. At first Susan found Anne moody and abrasive—"just another drunk," she said. "And at that point I was tired of drunks." (Susan herself never drinks, not even beer.) As the visit wore on, though, a certain rapport bloomed between the widow and the eldest daughter, one that owed, perhaps, to the streak of stubborn independence that ran through both women. After Susan flew back to Dallas, she stayed in touch with Anne, who made a point of keeping her abreast of all developments concerning her father's estates, both financial and literary. There was very little money, and very little likelihood of any money in the future, given that it was on the new book,

138

the lost book, that Boyd's publisher had been staking all its bets. Now, without the impetus that *Gonesse* was supposed to provide, the first two novels lapsed out of print. There were debts. Nonetheless the affection that had sprung up between Anne and Susan intensified. They spoke frequently over the phone; once Anne even came to Dallas for a visit, bringing along Bruce, who had to attend a conference there. When she arrived, Susan was surprised to discover that Anne had quit drinking and smoking, and lost quite a bit of weight. She now had the leathery, weather-beaten aspect—a sort of beauty— that you see in women who have spent too many hours in the sun. Her voice, though it remained raspy, was higher, more girlish. It was during this visit that Anne introduced Susan to Bruce, and told her of her impending remarriage. Neither Bradley nor Karen had any wish to meet her. She also said that she had just lately rewritten her will, naming Susan executor of Jonah Boyd's estate upon her own death.

So the bond was established. When the Ridges moved to Florida, Susan—tired of Dallas—decided to follow them. Her mother had recently died. She, too, felt ready for a change, and being an orphan, saw no reason why she shouldn't, as it were, "adopt" the Ridges as her parents. They were no longer young. Although Bruce had children from an earlier marriage, none of them lived nearby; two were in California and the third, amazingly enough, in Katmandu. Also, through her former husband, Susan had made some lucrative investments in the stock market, and had a little money to spare. So she quit her job, packed up her kids, and bought a house in Tampa, where she found work at a law firm. She tried to visit the Ridges every weekend. Not only was she growing ever closer to Anne, but also to Bruce, whose departure from

Kansas, she soon learned, had been hastened by something far less benign than a simple desire for better weather. For it seemed that one of the cloverleafs Bruce had designed had collapsed, due to a structural defect, killing seventeen people. Bruce could not reconcile himself to the idea that what was in essence a mistake in his own calculations had cost these people their lives. He gave up his work, gave up teaching. In Tarpon Springs, he grew increasingly absentminded, and spent as much time as he could sitting on the shores of lakes and sinkholes, painting burnished tropical sunsets and water-scapes in which alligators and manatees figured prominently. He painted flame trees. He painted snarky woodlands. Florida kitsch. So childlike had Bruce allowed himself to become that when Anne was diagnosed with lung cancer, she elected not to tell him, though she told Susan. The cancer, it seemed, was of a particularly pernicious variety; to combat its inevitable spread, her doctors were counseling surgery—removal of one lobe of Anne's left lung—to be followed by intensive chemotherapy and radiation. But Anne would have none of it. Of late she had been studying alternative therapies: herbal remedies, acupuncture, and Chinese medicine. She started taking ginseng, Echinacea, and vitamin E in quantity. Then one night she had a dream in which a voice speaking from a turtle's mouth gave her instructions as to how she could cure herself. Following the turtle's directions, she temporarily left Bruce, and rented a small cottage on stilts on the Atlantic coast, near Saint Augustine. It was July. Every day Anne lay on the beach in her bikini, a wizened woman of sixty-five who would rise from her sun worship once an hour only to wade out into the tide carrying a little plastic telescoping glass, which she would dip into the sea. Then, while the other beachgoers gaped in amazement, she would gulp down eight ounces of seawater. For this was what the turtle had prescribed. Every day for three months Anne lay in the sun, and drank glassfuls of the Atlantic. And at the end of this period, when she returned to Tarpon Springs, what did the skeptical doctors discover? That the cancer had gone into remission. The bizarre cure, for reasons that remain inexplicable, had worked.

After that Anne lived for five more years—far longer than the six months she had been given when her doctors made their initial prognosis. During that time she never once submitted to any conventional treatment. After she died, Bruce suffered several small strokes. His memory was sketchy: Though he could recognize, for example, the faces of his own children, as well as photographs of his wife, there were many days when he had no idea where he was. After a bizarre accident in which he nearly ran down a poodle, he lost his driver's license. Susan continued to visit him every weekend. She brought her daughters. Marching into his house on a Saturday morning with her retinue and a bag of groceries, she tried to be a reminder that even for an old man who was responsible for seventeen deaths, life could still contain many pleasures. She would cook him a good meal and then drive him out to the lakes he so loved, and which he could no longer get to on his own. Then he would sit on the shore and work on his paintings. Only when it came to painting had Bruce retained any of his old sharpness; brush in hand, he could at least achieve the clarity that eluded him in the negotiations of ordinary life. A hideous clarity, but a clarity nonetheless. It was during one of these visits—they had just returned from the lake, her daughters outside in the pool—that I called, and Susan answered.

We have spoken many times since then. On two occasions, she has visited me in Wellspring. I have visited her once in Tampa. Next month we plan to take a vacation together in Hawaii. Susan is a tall, leggy woman inclined to wear bold colors and big hats, the sort of woman often asked to give inspirational speeches to underprivileged girls. (At least, she was asked to give such speeches before the stock market crashed and her fortune shrunk to nearly nothing, obliterating her independence.) In her upright stance, if not in her demeanor, she is the spitting image of her father.

It was, I suppose, as much for her sake as for the sake of truth, or history, or whatever abstraction you wish to invoke—as much to ensure his daughter's future as to redeem Jonah Boyd's past—that I finally decided to confront Ben. By then two months had passed since I'd read *The Sky*. Ben had moved into his parents' house, and started teaching. Believe me or not as you choose: My intention, when I went to see him that day, was never to make ultimatums. My intention was merely to learn the truth. For I was not so foolish as to assume that what I assumed was necessarily what had happened. I only had the roughest sense of things. Nor had I said a word to Susan about my suspicions. I wanted to be sure before I did.

It was a Saturday morning in October. I didn't call first. I just showed up. The front door, not the back. When Ben answered, he seemed only mildly surprised to see me. He was wearing jeans and a blue Oxford shirt much like my own, only in his case untucked. He was drinking orange juice. "Denny," he said with a smile. And then he invited me in.

To start with, he gave me a tour of the house, as his mother had once done. The carpeting was gone; we walked on yards of oak herringbone parquet, buffed to a high gloss and still faintly redolent of polyurethane. Absent the gold-hued shag of the old days, the rooms seemed at once more elegant and less cushioned than I remembered them being. Otherwise Ben had done a remarkable job of re-creating the décor of his child-hood. The black leather sofa in the living room might have been the same one from which Jonah Boyd had held forth thirty years before; likewise the Danish modern chairs were the same, except that neither had cat pee on it. "Most of this stuff I found at auctions," Ben said, "and it cost a pretty penny. Much more than my parents paid for it when it was new. What fools Daph and I were to have sold it so cheap! Oh, and do you recognize the piano?"

I observed the fluted legs. Another Knabe. "That's amazing," I said. "It's almost identical."

"It's the same one. I tracked down the people who bought it at the estate sale, and they sold it back to me. And here"—he led me into the kitchen—"although this isn't the same tulip table, it's virtually the same. Nostalgia is expensive; this one cost nearly a thousand dollars. I don't know if you remember that Daphne kept the original. I tried to talk her into sending it back, but she won't."

I sat down. Aside from a new refrigerator and range, the kitchen looked pretty much as it always had, the only difference being that the cabinets, once robin's egg blue, were now yellow. "The Shoemakers were responsible for that," Ben said, "but I liked it, so I decided to keep it. Can I make you some coffee? Or would you prefer orange juice? It's fresh squeezed. I won't show you the study or the bedrooms because I haven't done anything there. I have to wait until I've got some more cash. Have to finish my book, and for the first time in my life, I've got writer's block. Can't write a word. Just looking at the screen gives me a headache. So predictable. As for the garden—well, if you look out the window, you'll see that where the koi pond used to be, there's this horrible sort of flagstone patio." He shook his head. "I could throttle Clark for that . . ."

He handed me a mug of coffee, then sat down across from me. As he did, I laid my copy of *The Sky* on the polar white surface of the table.

"I read this," I said, indicating the book.

His face remained placid. He looked as if he had been expecting this.

"I'm surprised you managed to find it," he said after a moment. "Copies are, to say the least, rather hard to come by."

"So I discovered."

"You were either lucky or tenacious."

"Both, probably. Did you take the copies from the libraries?"

"Libraries?"

"The university library and the town library. Both are missing."

"Some of my fans can be a little . . . well, overenthusiastic. Where did you get yours?"

"From the Strand."

"Oh, my old place of employment! Isn't that ironic? It fits, actually. It's all starting to fit."

"How so?"

"Just . . . the pattern." He leaned across the table. "So now you've got the book, and you've read it, even though I asked you not to."

"Correct."

"Okay . . . So what do you want? Have you come to blackmail me?"

It had never occurred to me that Ben might think I meant to blackmail him. Now I wondered if I did.

"But blackmail implies that I'm here to ask you to give me something," I said, "or do something, in exchange for my keeping quiet. And I'm not."

"Then why *are* you here?"

"Because I read the novel, and of course, from the first line, I remembered Jonah Boyd."

"What business is this of yours?"

"It's my business if I'm the only person to recognize the truth."

"And what truth would that be, pray tell?"

"That you stole Boyd's novel."

"Do you have any evidence to prove that?"

"No."

"Then why should I even dignify your charge with a reply?"

"But if what I'm saying is so ludicrous, then why did you instantly jump to the conclusion that I'd come to blackmail you?"

Ben turned away. It was a better question than I'd realized, for it silenced him. Suddenly I saw that he had no program, that he was winging it, changing his tactics entirely in response to what he was able to deduce, from what I said, of what I knew. Guesses at how much I had guessed. Which meant that the calm demeanor with which he had greeted my setting the book on the table was a pose. Under the surface he was quaking.

"No one will believe you. Why should they?"

"It's not as if there aren't other people who were there that night. Glenn Turner, for instance. Or Daphne. From what you've told me, you're not her favorite person right now. And of course, we have no idea who else Boyd read his chapter to."

"For someone who claims not to be a blackmailer, you certainly sound like one."

"I'm just pointing out that you're wrong to assume I'd have to have hard evidence to get people to take me seriously."

"Okay, fine. But you still haven't told me what you want. You've got to want something."

"Just an explanation."

"What's your hunch?"

"That you stole the notebooks."

"I didn't steal them."

"Okay, then that you found them, after the fact, and just . . . failed to give them back."

"That's not what happened, either."

"Then what did happen?"

He slapped himself on the forehead. "Oh, all of this is my own fault, my own lunacy! I've set the dogs on myself. I must have wanted to, somehow. Otherwise why would I have told you not to read *The Sky*, which is tantamount to saying, 'Read it! Read it!'? I guess I was afraid. It all seemed too good to be true. Back in Wellspring, a great job . . . the only trouble was, you were still around. That was the first thing I checked. I found out you'd retired. I hoped you'd moved away. But you hadn't."

"No."

"Of course all along I worried about you figuring it out. You, or someone. But as time went by, and nobody said anything, it just seemed less and less likely that anyone was ever going to. And then, fairly quickly, the book faded into obscurity. And now I come back, years and years later, and lo and behold, here you are on my doorstep with the damned thing in your hand . . . Well, it figures you would have found one of the only damn copies floating around. Remember what I said when we had dinner about predestination? About how my getting this job, my getting this house, all seemed like part of some plan? I still believe that—only now I'm not so sure that the force behind the plan was benevolent. Maybe the point was to ruin me, to punish me. I mean, look—here I am, where I've always wanted to be, and I can't write a word. And now here you are, with that book."

"You seem to have totally forgotten Jonah Boyd. It could be argued that the loss of his novel was what killed him."

"Anne never believed that. We spent a lot of time together, when I was at Bradford. He was dead by then, of course. You know, that was one of the principal draws of Bradford for me, the chance to take a workshop with Boyd, but he died the winter before I started. Still, I hung out with Anne. We talked."

"What did she say?"

"Just that he jumped on the bottle so fast, she didn't believe it was *only* because of the notebooks."

"Did you know that Anne is dead? I spoke to Boyd's daughter."

"Oh, you've really done your homework! Which one?"

"Susan."

"Yes, Anne was closer to Susan than to the other one."

We were silent for a moment, as if to honor Anne's passing. I noticed that Ben's glass was empty. He was drumming his fingers against its surface. And then, quite suddenly, he got up, in a way that startled me. What was I afraid of, that he was going to pull a pistol out of his pocket, grab a knife from a

147

drawer, and lunge at me with it? Nothing like that happened. "Follow me," he said, and left the kitchen.

"Where are we going?"

"I want to show you something."

I rose. We crossed the front hall into the bedroom wing, then walked to the end of the corridor, where he opened the door to the room that had once been Daphne's. It was dark in there; all the shades were drawn. I could make out a clutter of shapes, obstructions that Ben had to navigate as he made his way to the window. He pulled up the blinds, admitting some pretty, dappled fall light.

Then he beckoned to me. I stepped inside. Surrounding him—piled everywhere, on the bed and on the floor, in boxes in the corners and spilling out of the closet—were copies of *The Sky*. Thousands of them, all with that familiar cover, the zipper splitting the blue, the rain beneath. Everywhere there were tottering mountains of *The Sky*, stacks so precarious I wondered that they didn't collapse, and conical mounds like funeral pyres.

"You see?" he said. "For years I've been collecting them. Every copy I could find. So far, I've got about fifteen hundred, and given that the print run was thirty-five hundred, of which another fifteen hundred were returned to the publisher and eventually pulped, that means there are five hundred copies unaccounted for. Some are in libraries. Most are probably moldering on the bookshelves of people who have no idea they've got anything of value. And of course the value's been exaggerated, it's inflated, as a result of my hoarding. Most of the names on the waiting lists at the used bookstores—they're mine. Pseudonyms. I try to keep in touch with the major ones. The Strand's never supposed to sell a copy to anyone else.

When you called there, you must have gotten someone new who didn't know the rules. And yes, I admit, I have stolen a few from libraries, which I don't feel too good about—but when you think about it, it's so incredibly easy to steal a book from a library; all you have to do is slice out the security tag . . ."

"How long have you been . . . doing this?"

"Oh, for years. Since I published my second book. I really hoped that someday I'd manage to get them all, and then I could have a huge bonfire . . . What luck that you, of all people, should have gotten hold of one of the very few that aren't here in this room."

Clearing a space on the bed, Ben sat down amid his bounty. "You know, I've never talked about this with a living soul, except Anne," he said. "Not with either of my wives, never, God knows, with my parents—and now here we are on this lovely autumn morning talking about it, and you know what's surprising? It feels completely inevitable. I'm not even nervous. I'm kind of serene. I suppose there's some relief to be derived from being found out, especially after so many years. And who knows, maybe things would have been better in the long run if I'd been found out earlier on. Of course I wouldn't be here. I wouldn't be back in Wellspring. But that might have been a blessing."

He lifted his hands from his lap, ran his fingers through his hair. "I tried to write about this once. When I was working on the memoir. Now's my chance, I thought, I'll come clean, and people will be so amazed by my honesty, they'll be so humbled by my willingness to confess entirely for the sake of art, and not just because someone's found out or started hounding me, that they'll forgive me completely. Then I'll really be free. I won't have this thing nagging at me all the time. So I sat down to write the chapter, and I could only come up with two sentences. Two sentences, and such good ones! And then I lost my nerve. You want to know what the sentences were?"

"What?"

" 'On Thanksgiving Day, 1969, a woman decided to teach her husband a lesson. She enlisted as her accomplice a boy of fifteen who had ideas of his own.' "

"I don't understand. What woman?"

"Anne, of course. That's what no one would ever guess, if they tried to put the thing together on the basis of the circumstantial evidence. Yes, I stole Jonah Boyd's novel, and published it as my own. But I didn't steal the notebooks. Anne stole the notebooks."

"Anne?"

"You sound surprised."

"I am."

"I guess I might as well tell you the whole story. It'll take a little time. Do you want to use the toilet first?"

I did. As I peed in the bathroom that joined Daphne's room to Ben's, I wondered if he was sneaking out of the house, going back to the kitchen to fetch that knife. Part of me fully expected, when I emerged, to find him waiting for me, knife in hand.

Instead he was sitting just where I had left him, on the bed. He had cleared a space for me next to him.

I sat down, and for about two hours, he talked.

Eleven

I SHALL NOW report, as faithfully as I can, everything Ben told me that afternoon. I shall put the words in his own voice, in an effort to preserve his tone of confession. He called me his blackmailer, and in a sense, I suppose I am. Yet what is a blackmailer if not the very embodiment of conscience? Extracting a price for silence is not really that different from offering to absolve, in exchange for assigned prayers, a sinner's blemish. The blackmailer is not really that different from the priest. Nor is he necessarily an enemy. He can be a friend, too—the only person in the world in whom his victim can confide. This was certainly true in Ben's case. As he talked, his face itself seemed to open; the muscles of his brow relaxed. Not that he was proving his own innocence—far from it—but he was telling the truth, and something about that very gesture of honesty, after so many years, seemed to calm him. By the time he was done, Ben was a different man.

Here is what he said.

I've often wondered, when or if I ever told his story, how I'd structure it, where I'd begin, whether I'd withhold certain details until the end to build suspense, or spill it all, as it were, from the beginning. This is the usual writer's dilemma. I'm still not sure what I'll do, only I know that before I elucidate what actually happened that Thanksgiving, I first have to tell you something about Anne.

She was a very strange woman, in some ways seductive, in others weirdly repellent. Even when I was a little boy back in Bradford—you may remember her mentioning this—she used to give me massages. I mean, here I was, nine years old or something, and every time my parents had a party she'd be sitting down next to me on the couch offering to give me a back rub. Nine years old! And when she gave me those back rubs, I have to say, there was something in her touch that was much more than motherly. That was frankly erotic. Not that she ever touched my dick or anything; she'd just, now and then, run her fingers very lightly over my arms, so lightly that the hairs stood on end; or she'd let her hand dip for a second down to the waistband of my underpants. I won't pretend I didn't enjoy it. In fact, as I got older, I started to look forward to her coming over, because I hoped that when she did, she'd give me a massage. She didn't always. It was really a question of her mood, or how drunk she was. Once I hit puberty I even started plotting how I might get her alone, because I was convinced that if we could just be alone together for a while, she'd go the whole nine yards and jerk me off. That was as far as I let my fantasy go. I never imagined her blowing me, or my fucking her. I had my first orgasm thinking of her giving me a massage, reaching under the waistband of my shorts and touching my prick. Just touching it, very lightly. That's still such a potent scenario for me I've paid prostitutes to enact it. It's funny, I've had a fairly rich sexual life, I've had lots of experiences with lots of different kinds of women—and yet even today, nothing excites me more than getting a massage from a woman who's older than me. And now it's almost comical, because as *I* get older, the woman has to get older, too, in order to make the thing work. Which means, what, that when I'm eighty, I'm going to have to find a woman who's a hundred? And when you think that when all this started, Anne was younger than I am today . . .

Then we moved away from Bradford. I entered puberty. My voice changed.

In Wellspring, I started noticing girls at school. There was no question but that with their firm breasts and flat stomachs, they attracted me much more viscerally than Anne ever had. Still, she'd left her mark on me. For instance, after Mark went away, I was plundering in his closet one day when I found a copy of *Hustler,* which I started masturbating with. There were naked women with their legs spread, but there was also a sort of *tableau vivant,* a photo narrative, involving an older woman and a male prostitute. In the last photograph, the prostitute washes his genitals in the sink while the woman lies on the bed in fishnet stockings and garters, smoking a cigarette. I used to gaze at that photograph for hours. Hours. I studied it. I thought about Anne. The woman in the picture— her eyes had that same look as Anne's, a look of dissipation and the temporary abolition of a hunger, but not of any real satisfaction. And also recklessness, as if there were nothing she wouldn't try once,

I still have the magazine, by the way. I can show it to you any time you like.

And then one day, rather out of the blue, my mother announced that Anne would be coming to visit us over Thanksgiving, with her new husband.

Well, as you can guess, the news of her imminent arrival

provoked a violently mixed reaction in me. I was scared and excited at once. I wondered if she'd pull the old massage trick again, and if she did, if I'd still want her to. I was pretty sure I did—and yet a part of me worried that there was something wrong with wanting that, that I ought to be wanting only to get to third base, as we used to say, with Angela Longabaugh. And then when Anne did show up, the fact that she looked so awful—you remember, so sort of blowsy and bloated—only addled me the more. Because even with her looking like that, the fantasy hadn't lost any of its intensity, and by this point I was so obsessed with the fantasy that Anne's condition hardly mattered. Or rather, it mattered only to the extent that Anne was the conduit of the fantasy. Does that make sense? She could have weighed three hundred pounds and had boils, and still it would have had to be a massage, it would have had to be Anne. Once it had been lived out, I could forget it, forget her. But I had to get it out of my system first.

And then there was Boyd. I have to be honest, from the get-go, his presence flummoxed me. Whereas Clifford was this big guy, a real football-player type, but also sort of distracted all the time, not quite there—the kind of guy who chronically buttons his shirt wrong—Boyd was so perfectly put together it was scary. Also, he had this way of smiling at you that creeped you out and excited you at the same time—a sort of childlike grimace, inane, yet also hypnotic. I'll be honest with you, I thought he was a handsome man. Somehow he didn't look like a writer. For one thing, his posture was perfect. Whereas most of us have bent spines and flabby asses from sitting all these years at desks, his back was as straight as a ruler. And he smelled good—not like cologne, more like spices. Cloves, cinnamon. He smelled just like those goddamn notebooks.

Everything about him was clean, even his mustache, which always looked as if he'd just shampooed it. He was so gentlemanly, I think it rather floored my mother. Those weren't years when it was fashionable to espouse chivalry or decorum. Men were supposed to let it all hang out, while a woman, if a man opened a door for her, she was supposed to belt him in the chops. In this regard, Boyd was totally anachronistic, and if he got away with it, it was because he was something else, too: He radiated this intense virility that women responded to almost without fail. My mother certainly did.

Anyway, you can imagine how stunned I was when he took such an interest in me. I mean, you have to understand, at this point, in terms of my writing, no one, except maybe my brother, had ever given me even the slightest hint of encouragement. I was really on my own. My mother tried, but there was something so automatic about her praise, I couldn't take it seriously. My father just corrected my grammar. Boyd, though—from the minute he found out that I wrote, he treated me like a real writer. And this was fantastic, addictive. He talked to me about my poems in a way that implied he was actually interested in them, not just humoring me. And when I got to read aloud after him—well, I only wished Mark could have been there, because he would have been glad in a way that the others weren't. Mark was always good to me in that regard.

Of course, the poem I read was crap. I don't have to tell you that. Even so, Boyd applauded, and because he applauded, my mother did, and then everyone else. And then after I had finished, it was as if he was so high on the whole thing, he just wanted to keep talking about writing, so we went to my room.

He took his shoes off. I remember I put Joni Mitchell's album *Clouds,* which I'd just gotten, on the record player and then took it off again immediately, because how could we discuss literature with Joni Mitchell wailing in the background? Also, it had suddenly occurred to me that my fondness for Joni Mitchell might impugn me in his eyes, make me seem less like an authentic poet. So I put on a recording of the *Enigma Variations* that Mark had given me instead. This was the only classical album I owned.

We sat on the floor and—well—he tore my poem apart. I mean, just tore into it. He exposed everything that was wrong with it, every technical infelicity, every tonal misstep. Nothing got past him. He pointed out where I was bombastic and where I overwrote. And then, after he'd raked me over the coals, he showed me the lines (there were maybe three) that he actually thought were good, that in his opinion suggested I might really be a poet. Of course, coming from anyone else, I would have found that kind of criticism infuriating. I would have rejected it out of hand. But Boyd, because he wasn't just giving me unmitigated praise, the way my mother did, because he actually seemed to have thought about the poem, I had to listen to. It was really kind of exhilarating. And of course his instincts were unbelievably sharp. It wasn't at all like being told by my father, "You use *lay* where you should use *lie* in the third stanza." It was more like being told, "This line has life in it, this one doesn't." And then, as soon as he'd told me, of course I saw that he was dead on target. And so I took him absolutely at his word. It was the real deal.

There was something exciting about just sitting next to him, something warm and alive and responsive even in his posture. The thing about Boyd—I've thought about this so much since!—is that he might have been the most physical human being I've ever met. That's not very precise. What I mean is, in him the whole body/mind duality seemed to melt into irrelevance. Even his name was an anagram for body! And when he wrote, it was as if the prose poured, literally, from his fingers. The notebooks were amazing in that way. He barely ever revised, or deleted anything, or even crossed anything out. The prose just—well—*flowed*. He wrote the way most of us piss! The way he described it, writing, for him, was akin to going into a trance, and then transcribing what he heard. Yes, he did research—but not nearly so much as you might think! Later, when I read his books carefully, I found mistakes everywhere—factual errors, misquotations and misattributions, a thousand little inaccuracies that seemed so lame I could hardly believe he'd let them slip by. For instance, in *Gonesse*, he has someone meet Proust at a party three years after Proust died. He mixes up Schubert with Schumann. He even says the Champs-Elysées is on the Left Bank! The problem wasn't that he wasn't well informed—he read an enormous amount, and he actually knew much more about European history than I do—but he never took notes. He relied on his memory, which was, to say the least, fallible. And because he radiated such self-confidence, and the package was always so well put together, his editors never questioned him or checked up on him for accuracy. They took it for granted that he knew exactly what he was talking about. We all did.

In any case, to get back to Thanksgiving night—we were sitting there, Boyd and I, he'd just finished reading from his novel and we were listening to "Nimrod" a second time through (he had his eyes closed and he was smiling in that blissed-out, slightly goofy way of his) when suddenly there

157

was a knock on the door. It opened, and Anne walked in. She looked at us, and she said something like, "Come on, Jonah, it's time to go to bed," and dragged him up off the floor. I wasn't sure how I felt about that—on the one hand, the way she just barged in like that reignited the massage fantasy, because it made me wonder if she might come back in the middle of the night when I was alone. But she was also putting an end to an experience that was for me as close to sacred as any I'd ever known. I sensed that Boyd resented her interrupting as much as I did. "Good night, Ben," he said, "it's been a pleasure talking with you. Perhaps we can talk more tomorrow." I said, "Good night, Mr. Boyd. Good night, Mrs. Boyd." Then they went out, shutting the door behind them.

And here's the thing: *He left the notebooks*. I was going to chase after him, but their door shut, and then I heard them talking in what I can only call loud whispers. Arguing, I think. So I decided to wait and give him back the notebooks in the morning. I got into bed. The light in the bathroom came on and someone walked in. I heard water running from the taps, whispering, a toilet flushing—all those intimate sounds of a couple sharing a bathroom, sounds that other people shouldn't ever hear.

I remember that you stayed at the house that night. You were gone when I woke up the next morning. I suppose my mother must have hustled you out early. When I came into the kitchen, the Boyds were sitting with her at the tulip table, drinking coffee. Anne was in this rumpled housecoat, what my Jewish grandfather would have called a *shmata*, whereas Boyd—well, you can probably imagine how Boyd would have been dressed: He had on a sort of old-fashioned paisley patterned dressing gown, with a tasseled cord around the waist, slippers, and, if you can believe it, an ascot. I don't know where my father was—at school, or out in his office, seeing a patient. He saw patients at the oddest times, Sunday evenings, or at six A.M. Daphne must have still been asleep. I poured myself some cereal, and sat down with them, and everyone started asking me if I'd slept well. Then my mother said she had a favor to ask me. Because she and Anne wanted to practice, she wondered if I'd mind "taking care" of Mr. Boyd for the afternoon. That was the phrase she used— "taking care." And I said that of course I'd be glad to. Why not? I longed for more time with him.

So then my mother and Anne headed off to the piano, and Boyd and I got dressed, and met again in the study. "You left these in my room," I said, handing him the notebooks.

He looked at them as if he hardly recognized them. "Did I?" he asked.

I nodded.

"Oh, thank you, then," he said, and took them from me. "But don't tell Anne. She'd kill me. This will be our little secret."

We went out onto the back porch and then walked down into the garden. It was a gorgeous morning. You could see almost all the way to the Pacific. You don't get mornings like that much anymore. Boyd now had his notebooks—it seemed that he carried all four of them with him everywhere—and I had this sort of blank book in which I wrote poems and pasted pictures I'd cut out from magazines—psychedelic drawings, photographs of Joni Mitchell. Sixties shit. I'd bought it at the hippie shop on Connectisota Avenue. And Boyd was very curious about this book of mine, I guess because it reminded him of his own notebooks. So I took him down into the barbecue pit, which was my favorite place in the garden, and we sat together on that sort of built-in brick bench thing and flipped through the pages of my book, looking at the pictures and the poems. He read them and critiqued them. Once again, he was very hard. Two he told me flat out to throw away. But one he really liked. He actually loved it. It was a very simple little poem, about an airplane landing. And this kind of confused me, because the truth was, I didn't think much of this poem at all—I'd just sort of dashed it off, unlike some of the others which I'd really labored over—but even so, I was absolutely prepared to trust him. The question now was, what more could I ask of him, or expect of him? Would he offer to send my poem off to some editor he knew at a poetry magazine? Would he write me letters of recommendation? If I sent him more poems after he got back to Bradford, would he consider it presumptuous, or let the poems sit on his desk and never read them? Or would he be glad? I had no idea. At that age, you tend to assume—at least I did—that the world is full of codes and systems that everyone but you understands perfectly. And not only that, but that everyone else assumes that you understand those systems just as well as they do. And rather than admit your ignorance, you feel obliged to pretend you're completely at ease, when in truth you're completely at sea. What was going on here? What were the rules? *Were* there rules?

It was nearly noon. Off in the distance I could hear the piano—my mother and Anne hammering away at something, the way they did every Saturday morning. Oh, I'm sorry, that was you. And farther off, Ken Longabaugh raking leaves. And a car rounding the bend. It was odd—every noise that came to me was so much itself that today I can remember precisely what the world sounded like that morning, even though it was thirty years ago. The birds and the dryer tumbling. And then Boyd arrived at the last page of my little book, and closed it, and laid it on my lap. He looked me in the eye. I was too embarrassed to meet his gaze.

Very gently he put his arm over my shoulder.

"So what would you like to do this afternoon, Ben?" he asked.

I had a terror of tests in those days. I've never done well on them. Standardized tests especially were a nightmare for me, because they always seemed to represent a roadblock to my getting what I wanted—into the "mentally gifted minor" program, or into Wellspring. And now I was being asked a question for which I was sure I was expected to come up with some correct response, as in a test. And I was afraid that if I failed to come up with the correct response, I would somehow be cast out into the wilderness. Only I had no idea what the correct response should be.

That was when the idea of the arroyo hit me. At the arroyo, there was a lake with boats and nature trails that you could follow, and lining its perimeter were some good examples of thirties architecture. This meant that if Boyd wanted to sightsee, I could show him things. But if he wanted to talk more about my poems, or his novel, we could do that, too. So I suggested the arroyo, and to my relief, his smile broadened, and he said, "What a marvelous idea! We'll go in my car." My only clue as to how he hoped to spend his afternoon was that when lunch ended, and we got ready to go, I noticed that in addition to a Coke that my mother had given him, he was carrying the four notebooks.

Around two we drove down to the arroyo. It was one of

those beautiful autumn days that are bright but a little brisk, so that you have to wear your jacket but when you turn your face to the sun it warms you. We sat on a wooden bench, and he read some of his novel aloud to me—nearly the entirety of the second notebook. It took close to two hours. I kept waiting for him to stop, and he never did. Then when he got to the last page, he asked me what I thought, and when I told him I liked it, he must have taken this as leave to go on, because he immediately picked up the third notebook and started reading from that. By now I was about to go mad from restlessness. The sun was getting lower in the sky, and we were supposed to meet Anne and my parents for dinner at a Chinese restaurant, and I had to go to the bathroom. But he just kept on reading, never getting hoarse or needing water, utterly oblivious to my squirming, until finally he reached some dramatic juncture— the end of the middle section, I think—at which point he announced that he had to take a whiz and hopped up and went to look for a toilet. Even though I had to go too, I didn't follow him, for fear that I'd be pee-shy around him. Instead I crept into the woods and went against a tree.

When he got back, to keep him from reading even more— which he would have been totally capable of—I asked him how close he was to being finished with the novel. He said that he only had two chapters left to write—and then proceeded to explain to me, in excruciating detail, just what those two chapters were going to consist of, how he intended to tie up the different plot threads, the various denouements for which he'd already been making preparations, scattering little setups all through the book, the importance of which the end would thrillingly illumine. And as he talked, he got more and more excited. He even told me what he planned for his last line, which would be a repeat of the first line: *To make love in a balloon* . . .

It was one of the most frustrating experiences I've ever had. The more he talked, the less relevant I became. His interest in me was completely obliterated. He heaved forth all these ideas of his in this way that totally discounted my existence, and I became bored and irritated and, in a curious way, resentful. Not that I could have given him any more of my poems to read—I'd already given him all I had. Still, having been deprived all my life of that kind of attention, and then getting such a massive dose of it from Boyd, I thirsted after it more than ever. I wanted him to tell me again how wonderful my airplane poem was. But he just talked and talked about that goddamn novel of his, and as he did, I could see him gradually disappearing from the arroyo, from the bench, from me, becoming more and more remote from everything that had any physical reality, until it seemed that I could have gotten up and walked away and he wouldn't have even noticed that I was gone.

He had laid the notebooks down next to him. He seemed so totally unconscious of their presence there that suddenly I understood why Anne had gotten so furious at him upon their arrival. I wondered: When we got up to go to the Chinese restaurant, would he remember to take them with him? And if he didn't—if he just left them on the park bench —*then* what would I do? Alert him? Or just say nothing, walk away with him and see how long it took before he realized what he'd done? I have to admit, there was a part of me that was sorely tempted to stay silent. Something about that kind of obliviousness really brings out the sadist in people. Also, watching to see whether he'd forget the notebooks made for a kind of mesmerizing game: It was like a scene in a Hitchcock movie in which someone has left some crucial note in a hotel room, and the heroine is walking around picking things up and putting them down, and you're wondering if she's ever going to notice the note. But in the end, he didn't forget them. Oh, he did at first—he started to walk away without them—but then, just a few feet from the bench, he stopped in his tracks, stared into space for a minute, and ran back to retrieve them.

About the conversation at dinner that night I recall very little. I was in too bad a mood. I think I made a point of refusing to eat anything. I could be very difficult about food in those days. We were sitting at a round table with a lazy Susan in the middle piled with much more stuff than our group of five could possibly have consumed—kung pao chicken and lovers' shrimp and lo mein and a whole sweet-and-sour fish. There were a bunch of empty chairs, and Boyd had put his notebooks down on one of them. Now I watched them as I had in the park. Once again I wondered if he would forget them. Boyd himself was very quiet, as was Anne—maybe she'd been drinking—and my mother, in her usual way, was trying to fill up the silence with chitchat. She always felt it was her responsibility to keep the sociability flowing. And then we were finished eating, and the waitress took the masses of leftover food off to the kitchen to pack up. We opened our fortune cookies—mine, I remember, said, "Great things are in store for you"—and my father put his credit card on top of the bill, and my mother went off to the bathroom, presumably to claim a few minutes of tranquility and isolation for herself. Boyd still looked as if he was in another world. There was no more tea to drink.

Soon the waitress came to leave the boxes of leftovers and to take the bill and the credit card: A few minutes later she brought a slip for my father to sign. My mother returned, freshly perfumed. We all stood. And this time—I'll never forget it, Denny—this time it *did* happen, just like Anne had warned us: Boyd walked away from the table *without the notebooks*. And I just watched him. I waited for him to catch himself, as he had at the arroyo. I hoped he would. But he just strolled serenely toward the door. My parents went through, and so did he. Sailed through. The door shut behind them.

I turned around, to verify that the notebooks were still on the chair. They were. I looked at them, and as I did, it dawned on me that someone else was looking at them too: Anne. She raised her head, and our eyes met.

It was all over then. Because, you see, not only had she seen that Boyd had left the notebooks behind, she'd seen that I'd seen that Boyd had left the notebooks behind; and more than that, *she'd seen that I hadn't said anything.* Just as I'd seen that she hadn't said anything.

I think that at that instant a contract was sealed between us—one the repercussions of which, the real repercussions of which, I'm only now beginning to feel. They were all out in the parking lot, Boyd and my parents, and of course those notebooks might as well have been molten, the way they were glowing before us, there on the chair.

That was when she winked at me. It was the first seductive thing she'd done since her arrival. She winked at me, stole back to the table, picked up the notebooks—I was surprised they didn't burn her fingers—and shoved them into the enormous, shapeless handbag that she was carrying. "Don't say anything," she whispered. And then she grabbed me by the arm, and together we walked out to the parking lot, to the cars.

I rode home with my parents. My mother asked how my afternoon with Boyd had gone, and I said that it had gone fine. Then in the front hall she asked Boyd if I'd been a good host, and he said, "Tremendous," and then she asked what time he and Anne needed to get up in the morning, and if they needed her to wake them. He thanked her but explained that he'd brought a portable alarm clock. Anne was making a drama of stretching her arms and yawning, so we all said "good night" and headed off to our separate rooms. Boyd, so far as I could tell, still hadn't realized he'd left the notebooks at the restaurant, and Anne hadn't said a word to him about having grabbed them after the fact. I assumed she would tell him gloatingly, once they were alone.

"Sweet dreams," she said to me, as I drifted into my room—and then, for the second time, she winked at me.

"Good night," I said.

"Good night," Boyd said.

I didn't brush my teeth. I climbed straight into bed. The light in the bathroom went on, as it had the previous night; I listened to the now familiar sounds of conjugal ablutions. Then the light went off again. Their door to the bathroom closed. I hadn't locked mine—whether that means anything I leave it for you to decide. Now the house was silent, except for the pipes, which gave out occasional, comforting groans.

About half an hour later I heard a clicking noise. I sat up in bed. Someone had come into my room from the bathroom. This didn't in and of itself surprise me: On some level I must have expected a visitor from that quarter. The question was who the visitor was going to turn out to be—Anne or her husband.

It was Anne. Finger to lips, she sat down on the edge of my bed. As in the old days of the massages, she rested her hand on my stomach. She was wearing a nightgown as shapeless as her bag, which, strangely enough, she had also brought with her. She smelled of cold cream and cigarettes. Over my face she hovered, her hair pulled back and rubber-banded, smiling at me in that same dewy way that her husband had, and that had so rattled me. Perhaps she'd picked up the habit from him.

In a whisper, she started to talk. She talked almost as much as Boyd had, back at the arroyo. She told me that she was "fed up to here" with him. She told me that she often woke up in tears during the night, wondering if leaving Clifford and marrying Boyd had been a terrible mistake. Because, she said, almost from the day of their wedding he had ceased to treat her with affection. His work consumed him to such a degree that most of the time she felt as if she were merely a drudge, her duty in life to wash his clothes and make his bed and prepare his dinner. "And he can be violent," she added. "Oh, no one believes it, because in public he's always the perfect gentleman, not a hair out of place. He would never dream of making a scene in public. But then when we're alone, the smallest thing sets him off. This morning, for instance—I'd gotten dressed, and was getting ready to go play the piano with your mother, when suddenly he started . . . Well, just staring at me in this awful way that made my heart race. 'What's the matter?' I asked. 'I can't believe what a frump you've turned into,' he said. 'What are you talking about?' I said. 'You mean you haven't noticed?' he said. And then he laughed in this horrible way and said, 'If you can't see it for yourself, I'm not going to tell you.' I went into the bathroom and peered into the mirror, trying to figure out what was wrong. But I couldn't. So I went back into the bedroom and said, 'Please, Jonah, for God's sake, tell me what's wrong.' Then he made this noise of disgust, grabbed me really quite roughly by the arm, and dragged me back to the bathroom. And then he showed me, in the mirror, that there was this stain on my blouse. This really quite tiny little stain. And he explained very calmly that unless I changed my blouse, he wouldn't speak to me for the rest of the day. No one else would notice, he would do it so subtly; still, I'd feel it.

"I changed my blouse, and the whole time he lectured me about how fat I was, how I'd let myself go. He hated the first blouse I put on because it was wrinkled. He hated the second blouse because it didn't match my skirt. And on and on, until I didn't have any blouses left. 'Well, that last one will have to do,' he said, 'but really, Anne, this is absurd. You're an embarrassment.' And in the meantime my arm is aching, my right arm, because he's wrenched it so badly, practically pulled it out of the socket."

That same arm was now hovering over my diaphragm. Very casually—much as her husband had put his arm around my shoulder down in the barbecue pit—Anne started to touch me. She was talking and talking, and in the meantime her fingers were drumming my chest, darting now and then into the gaps between the buttons on my pajama top, brushing bare skin, once even tweaking a nipple. Of course, as you can imagine, I had a huge hard-on. How couldn't I, what with all the anticipatory tension of that long day, and now the prospect of Anne finally making the massage fantasy real? And so she went on touching me, and went on about how cruel he was, and how unhappy she was, and how could he have the unmitigated gall to claim that he cared about that novel more than anything in the world—even more than her—and yet be so cavalier as to leave the only copy in the world at a Chinese restaurant? So that on top of everything else, his abuse and his coldness, now she had this anxiety to contend with, feeling that she had to watch out for him every second. And all the while her hand circling, circling, getting closer to my groin. I was so hard my balls had nearly disappeared; I wondered what would happen if—when—she touched my dick, if I'd come right away, and in that case, whether she'd be pleased, or annoyed and frustrated. Once again, it was rules and systems, codes that I assumed everyone else understood perfectly, the outlines of which I could barely make out in the shadows . . . I wanted it all to be over, and at the same time I wanted it to last for hours, this sweetly awful hovering on the edge of an abyss that was somehow also a bridge over an abyss . . . and what was on the other side of the bridge? Part of my not wanting it to end was fear of what was on the other side.

She was careful. She knew what she was doing. She got close, then moved away. Prolonging the pleasure—the first hand other than my own. And in the meantime the monologue never let up. "But tonight decided me," she said. "What happened at the restaurant decided me. I've had it up to here with his recklessness. I'm going to teach him a lesson. But And I need your help."

Suddenly her hand stopped in its motions. I looked up at her. "Help?" I said.

You may recall that earlier I mentioned her having brought her handbag with her: that huge, shapeless handbag, so typical of its era, offering in its amplitude and ugliness a sharp rebuke to the little decorative pocketbooks of the fifties, those hard-edged patent-leather cylinders and shell-shaped clutches, designed to hold a Kotex and a lighter, that my mother carried with her to weddings. Feminism, in its early years, seemed to be all about refusals—to shave under the arms, to wear makeup, to wear a bra—and that handbag in a certain sense emblemized those refusals . . . Until that moment, when Anne lugged it up from the floor, I hadn't really registered the fact that she'd brought it with her on a journey that had required her to tiptoe all of twenty feet from her bed. Now, however, she was pulling the four notebooks from its depths; balancing them on my crotch, right on top of my hard-on. I was so close to coming, the weight of them nearly pushed me over the edge.

I looked at the notebooks. Never had they seemed so potent, so pregnant with . . . what? Malevolence? Promise? The very color of the leather seemed to have changed, to have taken on the hue of lava. I looked at them. And then I looked at her.

"I want you to do me a favor," she said. "I'm not going to give these back to Jonah. I want you to keep them."

"Keep them?"

"Hide them. And then tomorrow, when he wakes up and realizes that they're missing—*if* he realizes that they're missing—you're going to pretend you have no idea where they are. No idea at all. Everyone will go mad, your mother will tear the house upside down trying to find them. Still, you won't say anything. You'll even help her look. But you won't find them. No one will, because you'll have put them away somewhere no one would ever think of checking. Somewhere perfect. I leave it to you to determine the place. Somehow I suspect you already have a place."

"But why?"

"I told you. To teach him a lesson. It's not enough that he should be saved over and over, and always at the eleventh hour. If he's going to learn not to do this, he's got to really think he's lost them. And for a long time. A decent amount of time. Not just hours, or even days. At least a month."

"A month!"

"Or maybe two months. I'll decide all that. The point is, you'll be in charge of them. I couldn't have them in the house with me. It would be too risky. I'm not good at keeping things secret, the way you are. And so tomorrow Jonah and I will leave as usual, we'll head north, at some point he'll realize they're missing. Maybe we'll come back, maybe we won't. And then, when all possibilities have been exhausted, we'll go on to San Francisco without the notebooks, because he has this reading to give, and the show must go on, mustn't it? And the show will go on. And then we'll fly home. I'll see how he behaves, and if he's genuinely contrite, if I feel certain that he's learned his lesson and that from now on he'll start to act more responsibly, I'll get in touch with you. I'll call you or write to you. And that's when—miraculously—they'll turn up."

"But everyone will think I stole them!"

"No they won't. They'll all be too happy that you've found them. You'll be the hero."

"But how can I just *find* them? Where were they supposed to have been all this time?"

"That's immaterial. The point is, no one's going to think that you took them, because what would be the point of stealing them, keeping them for a couple of months, and then giving them back? On the other hand, finding them, purely by chance, in some corner of the house where no one ever thought of looking . . . that seems perfectly logical . . . Or you can turn them in, anonymously, to the police. I'm sure by that point Nancy will have notified the police." Anne's eyes, as she spoke, were glazing over. It was as if the plan itself, even on a hypothetical level, had so besotted her that for the time being the actual present moment had ceased to exist, much as it had ceased to exist for her husband that afternoon in the park, when he was talking about the unwritten final chapters of his novel. Meanwhile, under the weight of the notebooks, my erection was subsiding. Eros had fled the room, only to be replaced by forces less salubrious: greed, and dread, and vengefulness; possibilities of glory and of power, the power to control someone else's life, to make someone suffer, or flush with relief at your whim; and the power of knowing that the success or failure of a plan hinges upon your role, that you can sabotage it if you choose; and the power that naturally accrues to whoever holds a jewel or ring or amulet that has been endowed with magical proper- ties. For as you may have guessed, Denny, by now I was starting to view the notebooks themselves not merely as bargaining chips in some hideous game between husband and wife, but as objects in themselves capable of altering the course of human lives, for better or worse. Remember that Boyd, since his arrival, had been speaking of them in such hushed and reverent tones—implying, even by his habit of always losing them or leaving them behind, that they pos- sessed some mystic potency by virtue of which he could count on them always flying back to him of their own volition, like magic carpets. He had said, "I trust to the protection of the muse." If the spirit of the muse inhered, as this remark

172

implied, within the very leather and paper from which the notebooks were made, then it seemed logical that I—that any person who possessed them—would also come under the muse's benevolent influence.

My silence amounted to accord. Anne departed, creeping on tiptoe through the bathroom to her snoring husband's side, the bag that she carried now bereft of its contents, stretched and empty looking, like a condom thrown aside after an act of love. And I, in the meantime, was left with those four notebooks piled atop my groin. As soon as she was gone, I got out of bed and buried them in the chest where I kept the stuffed animals of my childhood. Amid Fatbottom the sheep and Gertrude the bear and the pajama bag in the shape of a turtle that Daphne had made me the Christmas when she had been briefly captivated by sewing, I thrust the notebooks containing Jonah Boyd's novel. They remained there all through the next day's search, and the next week, and the week after that, at which point I moved them to the place where they have remained, on and off, for the last thirty years. Have you guessed, Denny, where that is? Would you like me to show you? Come. Follow me.

Ben stopped talking. Standing from the bed, he went into his parents' bedroom, then out the door onto the back porch. As instructed, I followed. Down into the garden he led me, past the swimming pool and the flagstone patio where once the koi had swum, and then we made our way down the grassy slope into the barbecue pit. I don't think that until that afternoon I'd ever bothered to study the barbecue pit closely, not even during my fantasies of playing Dame Carcas. It was made of red brick; a chimney rose from its principal aperture, a sort of charred craw with a spit. Clearly one of the owners who had succeeded the Wrights had attempted at least once (probably a few times) to put the pit to the use for which it was intended, for as we neared it, I caught an unpleasant stench of wet ash. To the left and right of the aperture were two other openings, both much smaller, their blackened iron doors affixed to the brick by means of rather medieval looking hinges. "These must have been meant for storing charcoal or wood," Ben said, opening the one on the left. "When I was a kid I used to hide things here that I didn't want my mother to find, that copy of *Hustler* and my hippie book and . . . other things. Because she had an aversion to the pit, and refused to come down here. She was always bugging my father to fill it in, which he never did, probably just to spite her . . ." Soot blackened Ben's fingers. He reached inside the aperture, felt about for a moment, and then pulled out a lumpy parcel enclosed within a trash bag. This he handed to me.

"Open it," he said.

I took the parcel from him; untied the bag. Inside, individually wrapped in bubble wrap and carefully taped, were four books.

"Take one out," Ben coaxed, almost seductively, almost as if he were instructing me to undress him, one item of clothing at a time.

Because I keep my nails cut short, I had trouble catching the end of the tape. Finally, though, I got it going. The bubble wrap unfurled, revealing a familiar coffee-colored leather cover that still gave off a scent of cloves.

"Is this the first one?"

"Look and see."

I opened it; the pages had not even yellowed. *To make love in a balloon,* I read—and then I dropped the notebook onto the grass, my hands were shaking so, the coughs were rising so suddenly and so violently in my throat.

Twelve

HYSTERICAL ASTHMA, OR a reaction to breathing in too much soot: Call it what you will. Ben helped me back into the house, this time the living room, where he sat me on the black sofa. My hands were still shaking. After I had dropped the notebook, he had taken all four of them away from me and put them somewhere: I wasn't sure where. Now he stood near the fireplace, glaring, his face pallid with anxiety and surprise, as if my reaction to touching the notebooks—which was akin to what one might feel upon accidentally touching a corpse—had taken him totally off guard. Yet how could this be? Was it possible that he was recognizing only now, for the first time, the gravity of the crime in which he was implicated?

Very possible.

He watched me. He did not appear in the least to be in a state of denial. On the contrary, his eyes were hugely open. His lower lip drooped. He leaned against the mantel as if he required its support, as if otherwise he might fall. And then he almost did fall. I stood to catch him.

"I'm sorry," he said. "I haven't been feeling well lately. Headaches."

We returned to the kitchen, to the tulip table. I was better now, and told him so.

While he sat with his head in his hands, I made coffee. I found some bread in the refrigerator and toasted it. I found some margarine and some jam. We ate a vespertine breakfast, then, as the sun set outside the kitchen window. It was close to five-thirty, and still he had more to tell.

Here is the rest of it.

You're probably wondering what happened during the weeks and months after the Boyds left. Well, as I said, after a few days, I took the notebooks out of the chest with the stuffed animals in it and moved them to the place I just showed you, that little wood or charcoal store out in the barbecue pit. Having the notebooks in my room just made me too nervous. Not that my mother habitually went into that chest, or even opened it; and yet every now and then a sort of euphoria of cleaning would claim her, and when that happened, nothing was off-limits; there were no more hiding places; the house was forced to yield up all its secrets to her exhaustive vacuum. The barbecue pit was safer, I decided, both because it was outdoors and because my mother hated it so much she never went near it. She was the one who told everyone that the chimney didn't draw, yet so far as I'm aware, we never once lit a fire in order to test it, so how could she know? In any case, I was fully prepared to take advantage of her irrational dislike of the pit, for it meant that there was at least one place on the grounds of that house where I could count on her never to venture.

Of course, I was very careful with the notebooks. First I wrapped them in tissue paper, then in aluminum foil, then in plastic wrap. Almost archival. I was determined that nothing should happen to them, that when or if Jonah Boyd got them back, he should find them as pristine as the day he had lost them. Not that I was entirely sure that I *would* give them back, once Anne asked me to; for as I said, I was starting to make a cult of the notebooks, to look upon them as talismans possessed of a power by means of which I might get certain things that I wanted more easily or quickly—freedom from my parents, and from the tyranny of their indifference, and success as a writer. I thought of myself as the hero in a fairy tale, the shepherd or goatherd to whose protection some high priest has entrusted a rare treasure. And I was determined to do my duty by that treasure. Perhaps it was the barbecue pit itself that was influencing me, with its resemblance to a medieval keep. We talked about that once, didn't we?

Sometimes, though, I took the notebooks out of the pit and brought them back to my room. Then I would unwrap them and pore over them, amazed by the elegance of Boyd's handwriting, and the—to me—really astounding fact that he appeared to have written *Gonesse* more or less without ever revising, or reordering the chapters, or even altering the sequence of the paragraphs. He barely ever changed a sentence. My manuscripts, on the other hand, were horrible messes, with lots of rearrangement of the stanzas, and places where words had been erased and rewritten and re-erased so many times that there were holes in the paper. The squalor of writing—which I've always thought to be universal—Boyd had somehow managed to bypass. This was how I came actually to read *Gonesse*—not in one or even two sittings but over a succession of evenings during which I scrutinized the notebooks in an effort to unlock the secret of Boyd's method. I read each paragraph dozens of times, until I reached a point where I knew the manuscript practically by heart. And I adored it.

Meanwhile I waited for the promised call or letter to come from Anne, and as the weeks wore on, I wondered what, when she did call or write, I'd say to her. Would I do her bidding and "find" the notebooks? Or would I ignore her, pretend I had no idea what she was talking about—in which case, I knew, she'd have little recourse to take, given that accusing me of theft would mean by necessity implicating herself? Every day I returned from school dreading a message of some sort; every day I was relieved to find that none had come, since silence from Bradford, at the very least, let me off the hook. It meant that I could postpone, day to day, the moment when I would have to make a choice.

It was very strange. Anne and Jonah Boyd had entered my life so swiftly, and then disappeared from it so completely, that in the wake of their departure my memory of that Thanksgiving weekend itself became unmoored; it took on the drifting unreality of a dream. Had any of it even happened? Had Jonah Boyd really praised my poems, and put his arm around my shoulder, and read to me for hours in the arroyo? And had Anne Boyd tickled my chest, and rested the stolen notebooks upon my crotch? And had those notebooks really remained in my possession? A dash down to the barbecue pit confirmed that they had: Touching them sickened me vaguely, even as it reassured me. At least I wasn't going mad. Even so, knowing that they were buried out there—these objects in exchange for which a man far away would no doubt have paid a very dear price—troubled me. Recently I had seen a movie on television in which kidnappers buried a girl alive, in a coffin with a limited supply of oxygen. I was very susceptible to horror movies in those days, and from that evening on, the terrible story of the buried girl and the reality of the hidden notebooks became mixed up in my imagination, until I found myself waking in the middle of the night, afraid that somehow the notebooks would suffocate, perish from lack of oxygen, as the rescued girl had not.

Not only was there no communication with Anne, there was no news of her. If my mother heard anything about or from the Boyds, she never told me. Nor did I ask. I didn't want to come across as overly curious.

Still, I thought about them. When I applied to colleges, I included Bradford mostly because, despite everything that had happened, I still rather worshipped Jonah Boyd, and when I didn't get into any Ivy League schools or even Wellspring, I comforted myself with the knowledge that at least this way I could take one of his workshops. I even took the bold step of writing him a letter and including a story I'd just written. And in fact he did write back to me after a few weeks, a very sweet, very sad letter in which he apologized for taking so long to respond, then explained that he'd been depressed of late because of losing his novel. As for the story, it was "marvelous"—that was all he said. There was none of the sort of detailed criticism that he'd given my poems when he'd come to visit. There was no *substantive* response at all, which annoyed me. Of course, he concluded, when I got to Bradford I would be welcome to take his class; he'd save a spot for me. But that was it. A letter of a paragraph, at most. And then just a month or so later, he was killed in that car crash. I still hadn't heard from Anne, and now I supposed I never would.

At first, when I started at Bradford, I made a point of trying to steer clear of Anne. I never went anyplace where it seemed likely I might run into her—supermarkets, for instance. (I suppose I assumed that because my mother spent so much of her life in supermarkets, Anne would too.) Early on I had looked up her address. She lived on Silver Avenue, in a neighborhood of older houses through which, under normal circumstances, I would have bicycled on my way from the dormitory to the history department, where I took most of my classes: It was the most direct route. In my mania not to run into her, however, I used to take a detour around the football stadium that added at least ten minutes to the trip—all so that I would never have to lay eyes upon the house where Jonah Boyd had lived, or upon the woman who lived there still.

Of course I heard news of her. Boyd's death was still so fresh that people gossiped about it, other students as well as professors and secretaries. Already rumors swirled of a lost novel. And there was gossip about Anne as well. No sooner was her husband in the ground, people said, than she had quit drinking and smoking. Cold turkey. She was said to have lost forty pounds; to have cut her hair short and stopped dyeing it. Someone saw her at the pool, swimming laps and talking to the lifeguard. What did this mean? Was she glad of her husband's death? Had she perhaps had a hand in it? And then one day—inevitably, in that small town—I did see her. I was riding past the library on my bike, and she was walking across the lawn that fronted the administration building. At first I barely recognized her, she was so changed. Not only had she lost weight, she was positively slender; you might have even said gaunt. Her hair was short as yours, Denny, and was a sort of glorious silver color. She wore a loose sundress and sandals.

Fearful in case she should recognize me—but was she even aware that I was now a student at Bradford?—I turned around and rode away from the history department, circling back only once I was sure she was gone. But the next day, when I biked to class, instead of going around the football stadium I took the more direct route, right down Silver Avenue, right past the house where she lived. From the outside, at least, it appeared to be a rather ordinary house, built in the forties, of red brick with green shutters out of which half-moons had been cut. There were roses in the front yard. The curtains were closed. A blue Buick was parked the driveway. No sign of Anne, though.

I felt curiously ebullient—as if, merely by bicycling by her house, I had conquered some demon in myself, or made the first step in some process by which I might undo the past. Suddenly I felt I no longer had anything to fear on Silver Avenue, and I gave up my old route round the football stadium. Now I rode boldly by Anne's house every weekday, every weekday I gazed frankly at the front door, almost willing her to step through it and look me in the eye. This went on for about two weeks—and then one morning, I actually did see her. She was standing on the front lawn in jeans and a man's oversized T-shirt, pruning her roses. I don't know what possessed me then: To my own surprise, I found myself slowing down, coasting, stopping. She looked up, and smiled.

"Well, Ben," she said without much inflection. "Long time, no see. What made you wait so long to come by?"

"You mean you knew I was here?"

"Of course. Your mother wrote and told me."

"I didn't know you werc in touch."

"Not often, but occasionally."

Putting down her secateurs, she wrapped her arms around

her waist, under her breasts. "Well, you've grown up," she said. "Every day you look more and more like your father."

"I wasn't sure you'd want to see me."

"Don't you mean you weren't sure you'd want to see *me*?" But then she smiled again, and invited me inside.

I couldn't go. I was late for class. Still, I let her press me into accepting an invitation to tea that afternoon. "Tea" seemed very unlike Anne. After my classes were finished I returned to the dorm, showered, changed my clothes. For some reason it seemed important that I make myself as presentable as possible. I arrived at her house like a suitor, or the son of an old friend pressed by his mother into service. I had bought flowers. Once again, she was wearing a sundress—a different one, red with large gold poppies on it. To my surprise she kissed me on the cheek, and then she led me inside.

From that day forward, Anne and I were friends—real friends—and during my Bradford years I visited her often. It turned out that the façade of the house—which she and Boyd had bought with the advance for *Gonesse,* just after their marriage—was deceptive; once you got through the door, depths of space were revealed at which the view from the street barely hinted. There was a big living room with lots of books in it, and also a sort of garden room that opened onto the backyard, with French doors looking onto a rose garden even more exuberant than the one in the front. This was where we would sit and talk on the occasions when I visited her. We'd drink tea, and she'd ask me about my life, if I had any girlfriends, how my writing was going. She never touched me, as in the old days. I wasn't sure if I was disappointed.

It took three of these little teas before the subject of her husband, and the notebooks, even came up. And when it did, she was the one who brought it up. I wasn't entirely sure that I was glad. After all, to talk about the notebooks was to admit that they were real, and now that Jonah Boyd was dead, the fact that I still had them in my possession, cramped within their brick prison like the kidnapped girl in the movie, made me more uneasy than ever. Left to my own devices, I probably wouldn't have ever said anything about them. But Anne was always braver than I was.

I remember that the weather was glorious that day. In addition to the tea, which was Earl Grey, and headily aromatic, there were cookies that she had baked herself. Oatmeal cookies. I loved oatmeal cookies. Under different circumstances—at home, for instance—I might have scarfed down the whole plate in a minute flat. Yet that afternoon I felt that I should be polite. No doubt this had something to do with Anne's amazing transformation from slattern into the shimmering, almost haloed creature who now sat before me. I took one cookie, ate it as slowly as I could, and looked her in the eye.

"So have you still got them?" she asked.

I pretended ignorance. "Got what?" I asked.

"The notebooks, of course."

I returned my attention to the plate of cookies. Nine remained.

For some reason I now felt that I could take a second cookie, and I did.

"Yes, I've still got them," I said after a bite.

"I suppose you'd like to know why I never got in touch with you."

In fact I didn't particularly. Still, I couldn't very well just tell her to cease and desist. So I nodded, and took a third cookie, and arranged myself into a posture of listening.

Though I can't be sure, my guess today is that I was the first person—perhaps the only person—in whom Anne ever confided any of it, the story of what had happened in the years between her visit to Wellspring and her husband's death. "No doubt once I'm dead, I'll rot in hell," she said very matter-of-factly, as she sipped that delicious tea in that beautiful garden room on that sunny afternoon, with the roses outside the window and those cookies enticing me from their plate. "But does that mean I shouldn't enjoy what's left of my life? I don't see why. Yes, I destroyed him. I murdered my husband. Not that I meant to. But at least *I'm* alive.

"I want you to know that it really was my intention, from the very beginning, just to teach him a lesson, to let him *think* he'd lost the notebooks and then, once he was good and sorry, surprise him with the good news that they'd been found. And then how happy he'd be, how grateful! As I must have told you, we weren't very happy together. Jonah really was the most selfish of husbands. Whole days would pass sometimes during which he wouldn't even talk to me—sometimes to punish me, but more often because he was just so lost in his writing that he couldn't bother to acknowledge the existence of another person's needs. And this made me sad. And furious. But then once the notebooks were lost—correction, once you and I stole the notebooks—everything changed. His entire personality changed. Back in Bradford he became not only docile, but genuinely affectionate—the way he'd been before we were married, when I was divorcing Clifford and our relationship was still illicit. Don't get me wrong: The loss made him wretched. He really had adored his novel, and genuinely believed it was going to be his masterpiece. Whether that's the case or not, I'm not sure. Maybe you can tell me, since no doubt you've read it by now."

She lifted her head, reached into her purse, and extracted what appeared to be a cigarette but turned out to be a little plastic cylinder posing as a cigarette—a faux cigarette. This she placed between her teeth.

"In any case," she continued, "I encouraged him to rewrite the novel from memory, and to his credit, he did try. In the old days it had been his habit to get up early and go to his office at the university to work, and now he resumed it. Sometimes I'd visit him there. From outside the closed door, I'd hear the pecking of the typewriter. He said he couldn't bear to write in the notebooks anymore, even though he had a whole stock of blank ones. They reminded him too much of what he'd lost. Instead he typed, and then went instantly to make copies—a vain attempt to compensate for his earlier carelessness, too little too late. But his heart wasn't in it, and despite his valiant efforts, he just couldn't replicate the magic of the original novel. I don't think any writer's ever succeeded in doing that. Rather, he said, it was like warmed-over meatloaf. Like eating warmed-over meatloaf, day after day after day. But what he had written in the notebooks, what he had lost, was the most divine elixir, nectar of the gods.

"Remembering him saying that makes me miss my husband. Although it annoyed me sometimes, the truth was, I rather adored his crazy, inflated rhetoric. It was part of what made him so appealing—this boy from Texas who talked like Longfellow. In any case, after a month or so he gave up on his effort to rewrite the novel. He said he was just going to rest for a while, focus on teaching. And meanwhile his editor—a new editor, because the old one had been fired—was breathing down his neck to get her the manuscript, because earlier he had promised to be finished by February, and so they had gone ahead and put *Comesse* into their fall catalogue. The publisher's catalogue. He kept putting her off, promising to have it to her the next week, and then the next. I don't know what he was thinking, only that he was forestalling what he saw as an inevitable and terrible confession, which would be tantamount to admitting to himself that the notebooks, and with them the novel, were gone for good. And of course I think he was also putting off facing the fact that what had happened would have some inevitable fall-out, that he might be asked to return the money he'd been paid, or fail to get tenure.

"Of course, this would have been the logical moment for me to call you, Ben. The pressure was really on—not only from Jonah's publisher but from Bradford. I should have called you then and told you to do your stuff, to find the notebooks. Then Nancy could have phoned me up joyfully to say she was holding them in her hands, the wayward children ready at last to be returned to their parent. And then I'd have told Jonah, he'd have been overjoyed, and arranged for them to be sent back the fastest way possible. And the old life would have resumed . . . Yes, in retrospect, I see that that's exactly what I should have done.

"So—why didn't I? Not a simple question to answer.

"Well, first things first. I was a drunk, and drunks never think clearly. And yet more to the point, in his new state of mourning and contrition Jonah had become, as I said before, loving and affectionate and seemed to need me in a way that he never had. But if he got the novel back, would he continue to? Wasn't it more likely that he'd revert to his old, ignoring ways?

Was there even any guarantee that he'd start taking care with the notebooks? I feared he wouldn't. It would have been the old life, and I didn't want the old life. Before, when he was writing, Jonah would bound out of bed early every morning, sometimes as early as five-thirty, to write. I hated that. I was a light sleeper, and even though I'd want to get up with him, usually I'd be too hungover to make it out of the bed. I'd listen to him bustling around in the kitchen, listen to the car pulling out of the garage, and then I'd just lie there in a sort of anxious delirium until nine or so, when I'd stagger out of the bedroom only to find the house so unbearably empty and lonely that I'd have to pour myself some gin and orange juice and watch *The Price Is Right*. But now, of course, he had nothing to get up for, no reason to bound out of bed, and so he'd stay with me every morning, sleep late with me—and not just lie in the bed, but hold me. We'd spend hours and hours like that. It didn't matter that we never had sex. The affection, the hugging and the languorous mornings—they more than made up for the lack of sex. Now he never found fault with how I dressed. He hardly mentioned how I dressed!

"I suppose you can guess what all this is leading to. One afternoon I came back from somewhere—the liquor store, probably!—and Jonah was in the living room, just over there, standing by the wet bar. You probably can't tell, but in that corner over there, that used to be a wet bar. Today I don't keep any liquor at all in the house, not even a bottle of cooking sherry, but back then we used to have every kind of booze you can imagine. Gin, vermouth, rum, whiskey, vodka, bourbon. And now Jonah, who had been dry for years, was standing at the wet bar, and methodically mixing himself a martini. He was doing it very professionally, too, almost like a bartender.

"He smiled when he saw me in the door. 'Lovely wife,' he said, 'I'm just making myself a wee cocktail. Would you care to partake?' Or something like that. And I just looked across the furniture at him.

"Something passed between us then. I knew he was considering his options very carefully. He wasn't a stupid man. He understood that if he had one drink, he'd have another, and then another. He put the gin and the vermouth into a shaker with some ice. And he shook. And the whole time he was gazing at me, cow-eyed, as if he were about to burst into tears. And then he poured the stuff into martini glasses and handed me one. We sat on the sofa. He said, 'Sometimes it's just too much, you know?' I nodded. And then we drank.

"There's not much more to tell. Things got bad very fast. He started showing up drunk to class, and was abusive to his students. One of them complained, and he nearly lost his job. But by then, of course, word of what had happened—the loss of the novel—had leaked out, or he'd confided it in someone, and the chair felt sorry for him. He let Jonah off with a warning.

"The ironic thing is, even though he could get in foul moods when he was drunk—dark, violent moods—still, I remember those last months before he died as among the happiest I've ever known. Never before had Jonah seemed so completely, so entirely in love with me. Nor I with him. We were husband and wife, but we were also what we had once been, illicit lovers, and we were also something new. Drinking chums. Drink really forges a bond. That's why drunks like to hang out together. And we were classy drunks. I remember going out to the bookstore one day and rather jauntily buying a sort of cocktail cookbook. We used to read it together in bed. We'd prepare all sorts of exotic drinks for ourselves, the way other couples cook. Frozen things, things in pineapples with little umbrellas. The most divine bloody Marys. And every day I'd think, 'Today I'm going to write to Ben and tell him to quote-unquote find the notebooks,' and every day I'd put it off. And why not? What I was postponing was the end to my own happiness, a weird, dreadful sort of happiness, but a happiness nonetheless.

"Of course it ended anyway. It had to. The day Jonah died, I had a presentiment that something bad was going to happen. The rain was coming down in sheets. We were out of vodka. I'd suggested he not risk driving in that bad weather, but the suggestion was half-hearted, because the truth was, I wanted the vodka as badly as he did. He headed off, and I waited here, in the garden room. I watched the rain falling against the windows, listened to it drumming the roof. He didn't come back, and he didn't come back. I got dozy. Abstractly I imagined a car crash. But it was all dreamlike. And then the phone rang. The police.

"The shock of what had happened woke me up to what a freak I'd grown into. I realized that I might die too, if I didn't change soon. Since that day I haven't had another drink, or smoked a single cigarette. I feel better than I have since I was a girl.

"Does this seem horribly callous to you? I want something decent for myself. Even though I acknowledge my crime, I'm not prepared to spend the rest of my days on this planet doing penance for it. What good could come of that? Two lives ruined, instead of just one."

She stood, picked up the tea things as well as the plate on which the cookies had rested. It was empty now except for a few crumbs. She put everything on a tray and carried it into the kitchen and then she came back, and sat down once again across from me.

That was when she said, "So what are we going to do about the notebooks?"

Thirteen

ANNE AND I stayed in touch for most of the rest of my time at Bradford. Not that we saw each other every day; on the contrary, sometimes weeks or even months would go by during which I wouldn't hear so much as a word from her, or think about her—and then one morning, rather out of the blue, an image of her face would pop into my head, and I'd feel compelled to bicycle by her house; knock on her door. She always looked the same: curiously fresh, almost innocent, as if everything she had endured and perpetrated, rather than etching lines of age and corruption into her skin, had some-how renewed her youth. Or perhaps, like Dorian Gray, she had some gruesome portrait of herself hidden away in a cranny of that deceptively big house.

It wasn't about sex. Sex never happened, or even came up. And though the massage fantasy lingered, at that point I wouldn't have even considered mentioning it to Anne. She seemed too pure for that now, and anyway, I had by this point imprinted my longing, as it were, upon other women.

Sometimes we talked about the notebooks. Anne was always the one who brought the matter up. It seemed feasible to her, she said, that even at this late date they might be "found" without either of us coming under suspicion—in which case, she proposed, I could perhaps finish the novel myself (hadn't Boyd told me his plans for the last chapters?) and she could send it to his editor, who could arrange for its posthumous publication. After all—out of kindness, she suspected—the editor had never asked that she return the money Boyd had been paid as an advance. A tax write-off, as well as a write-off to the conscience, saving the poor woman from having to live with knowing that she had forced Anne out of her home. This way, though, the debt could be erased, Anne said, in addition to which there was more money to be paid on acceptance of the manuscript, and even more to be earned from royalties— money, of course, that she would share with me. Divide with me. But I was wary of complying with the plan, not only because I feared, more than she did, being found out or accused of theft; also because it was becoming increasingly clear to me that only so long as I actually held the notebooks in my possession could I be sure of having any leverage with Anne. Yes, she had proposed that I could write the unwritten chapters—but who was to say there wasn't another writer who could have fulfilled that task just as well? And for all I knew, Boyd might have told her everything he'd told me about the last chapters. So I demurred, changing the subject or putting her off every time the topic came up. And what could she do, when I demurred, but accept it? In a sense neither of us could really afford to make a move without the other's cooperation—as long, that is, as the notebooks remained under my control. Once I gave them to her, on the other hand, she could easily double-cross me, either by doubting the miraculous coincidence of their suddenly turning up, or by going further and implying that I had stolen them—in which case I would be the one who had no recourse, as of course the notebooks would by then be in her possession. That wasn't something I was prepared to risk. So I stalled, saying things like, "I'll have to think about it," or, "I'm not quite ready yet." Nor was she pushy. In fact, I suspect that despite her insistent positivity, her determination to make the rest of her life as free of taint as the last years had been marred by it, some terrible guilt still plagued her. In some ways, to forget about the notebooks suited Anne as well as it did me.

Meanwhile, wrapped in foil and paper and plastic, they sat where I had left them, in their little cave. Whenever I went home, for Christmas or during the summer, I would check on them. Once or twice I removed them from their protective casing, examined them to make sure that no damage had been done by smoke or rain or mildew. Their resistance to the elements deepened my conviction that they possessed some sort of magical properties. For it seemed that no matter how many years they sat in that sooty chamber, each time I unwrapped them they still smelled as they had the Thanksgiving when Jonah Boyd had passed them around the table. They smelled like him—just as that Thanksgiving I had thought that he smelled like them.

Then I graduated from college. I moved to New York. Anne and I lost touch.

You must believe me when I say that it was not until many, many years later that the idea of publishing *Gonesse* as my own work even entered my head, and by then, of course, Anne was dead, and my father was dead, and my mother. I had written three novels of my own, none of which I'd been able to sell. Oh, I'd had bites. Editors are sadists, Denny. They love to say to a young writer, "I can't buy your book as it is, but maybe if you fix this, or alter that, I'll reconsider." And so you fix this, and alter that—you do exactly what the editor has suggested—and what's the reply? "Well, if it weren't for this or that, the novel would be perfect, but as it is, it's impossible, it will never sell." As you can imagine, after a while that sort of bait-and-switch can become really infuriating. And I got it again and again. Maybe things would have been easier if I'd just met with swift and merciless rejection from the start— then, in all likelihood, I would have gotten the message and given up—but now it seemed that I was doomed to be forever tantalized, to have a remote if real opportunity perpetually dangled before my eyes, only to be withdrawn at the last minute.

One editor in particular drove me crazy. She had the extraordinary name of Georgiana Sleep, and she worked for Boyd's old publisher. Indeed, she seemed kind of impressed that I had known him, and had won a prize named after him. The thing about Georgiana was that she wasn't just vaguely encouraging without ever making an offer; she actually seemed to go to great lengths to woo me. At first our relationship was strictly epistolary—enthusiastic, witty, occasionally flirty letters from her, to which I would write agonized responses that strove for cleverness—but then one afternoon, rather out of the blue, she telephoned. She had a thin, high voice. I had just sent her my second novel, and she was calling, she said, because she wanted to talk about it with me. She proposed that we have lunch. This was unprecedented. I thought I had it made. Excited by her interest, and in spite of her voice, I created in my own head a Georgiana who was Amazonian and beautiful, as well as hugely powerful; imagined that over the course of the lunch, over white wine and very refined fish, she'd tell me that she and her colleagues had been so bowled over by my novel that they were now prepared to offer me a staggering advance, at which point we'd toast the future, and my career would be made. I even splurged and bought myself a new suit just for the lunch, even though this was something I could ill afford. But then when I showed up at the restaurant, Georgiana turned out to be just this girl, this wisp of a thing, with long blond hair and a freckled nose. She didn't even drink. She was probably five years younger than I was. And the restaurant to which she had invited me—far from some glamorous haven of luxury like the Four Seasons—was a sort of hip lunch counter, with fifty kinds of soup on the menu. And so we sat there over split pea soup, and she proceeded to tell me, in excruciating detail, everything that in her opinion was wrong with my book, which was pretty much everything, and as she went on, all I could think was what a fool I felt in that suit, and was it too late to return it? What if I spilled soup on it? Molly, my girlfriend, was always nagging at me to get what she called "a real job." She worked for an advertising firm, and frankly, I think that my idleness— what she perceived as my idleness—embarrassed her. I'd trumpeted this lunch as the beginning of a new stage in my life, promised that after this I'd be able to take her on vacations to Lake Como, Fiji, Kyoto. Now I didn't want to contemplate how she'd react when I came home and told her that not only had I not sold my novel, I was out three hundred dollars for the suit.

Still, even as I prayed for the lunch to end, and for Georgiana to ask the waiter for the bill, I was holding out hope that perhaps she was withholding some surprise for the last minute—that as we stood to leave, she'd say, "Despite all of this, you're so promising we want to give you a contract." But all she said was,

"Despite all of this, you're so promising that we want to keep in touch with you, and hope you'll send us more of your work."

At least she picked up the tab.

Those were very difficult days for me. I'm not going to go into it, because it's all too depressing. Don't think that I had any illusions about my own writing. Hope and ambition in spades, yes—but if I'm to be perfectly frank, I knew that Georgiana was smart and right. My novels so far lacked some spark of life, that element of vitality that distinguished the work of all the writers I loved to read. It seemed to me in those days that whatever the formula was—whatever combination of literary prowess and instinct for the marketplace brought a writer recognition, and brought pleasure to readers—I just couldn't put my finger on it. Now, of course, I realize that there is no formula. I see that had I merely written what I wanted to write, instead of constantly trying to second-guess Georgiana and the other editors, I might have gotten further. That's what I do now—or did, until this damned writer's block—and people seem to love it. But when I was young, rather than writing for myself, or for some idealized, unseen, perfectly intelligent and perfectly ignorant reader—that retired schoolteacher in Chicago whom we writers are supposed to visualize when we work—I wrote for Georgiana and her mysterious, monolithic "we." Her editorial board. If I saw her as my one hope, it was because at this point she alone, of all the editors to whom I'd sent stuff, would answer my phone calls. And not only answer them, but answer them gladly. Molly was jealous of her. She referred to Georgiana as my "girlfriend," or to use a British parlance of which we were both fond (we spent an inordinate amount of time watching British sitcoms) my "bit of fluff." She might have been right.

Today it seems clear that, at the very least, Georgiana had a crush on me. The smartest thing I could have done, I see now, would have been to marry her, or at least screw her. In any case, by the time I got wise she was already married to another writer.

In the meantime the third novel wasn't going well at all, probably because I'd banked so much on it. Still, I managed to bring it to some kind of conclusion and rushed it off to Georgiana, who turned it down flat in forty-eight hours. "I just think you're on the wrong track here," she told me. Correct, of course—though not what I wanted to hear.

I decided right then that the problem wasn't with me. I convinced myself. The problem, I told Molly, was with Georgiana. In her youthful avidity for power, she was teasing me, toying with me, taking advantage of my hunger and inexperience to feed her own vanity. It seemed inconceivable, for instance, that she would treat an established author this way—that she would treat Jonah Boyd this way. But of course Jonah Boyd was dead, and in truth, I had no idea how Georgiana treated established authors. I didn't even really know whether or not she actually had the power to acquire books. It might have been a bluff. She might have been a glorified secretary, or the tout for a real editor who remained nameless.

It was around this time that my father was killed, and my mother summoned me back to Wellspring to help her conduct her battle to keep the house. Believe me, Denny, I was eager to go. New York oppressed me. Things with Molly had gone from bad to worse, her disapproval of my joblessness slowly eroding even the affectionate rapport that had grown up between us. I guessed that it would only be a matter of time before she found herself a new boyfriend, some lawyer or banker who owned his own apartment. So I went. Those were strange days—my mother and Daphne and her kids and me, all piled up under one roof, not to mention Phil's trial. But they were also curiously pleasant days, and if I remember them today with fondness, it is mostly because the campaign to keep the house, and not less than that, the arduous labor of nursing my mother through her final illness, distracted me from the awful chore of writing. I had other things to think about now, and for all the grief that I felt, I was more at peace than I'd been in years.

We lost the house, of course. My mother died. I thought for a time that perhaps the fact that my father had been murdered by one of his students—and on campus, no less—might dispose the provost to look favorably upon our cause. But it did not. Indeed, I think the provost feared that if he appeared to be offering anything in the way of compensation to Ernest Wright's widow, we might use that kindness as leverage to ask for more. The thin end of the wedge. So we sifted through all the records and books and furniture, divvied up what we wanted from what we wanted to sell, and got ready to move out. But you know all this.

It wasn't until the evening before the closing that I retrieved the notebooks from the barbecue pit. I did it under cover of darkness. No one saw me, though when I got back into the house, Mark, who was reading in the study, did ask me what I'd been doing outside. "Looking at the stars," I said. By now Mark was married to his Canadian and leading his Canadian life, and we weren't nearly so close as we'd been in the days when he'd been a draft dodger. He wouldn't even sleep in the house. He insisted on staying at the Ritz-Carlton, to prove his wealth, I guess. Still, it is the older brother's prerogative to interrogate the younger.

Since nothing held me to New York any longer, and since I could now afford, with my portion of the proceeds from the sale, to buy another house, if a smaller one, I asked Molly to marry me. I told her that we could live anywhere she wanted. It seemed that during the weeks I'd been away, she too had gotten sick of New York, if not of the hypothetical lawyer or banker who had been my replacement. A junkie had tried, rather ineptly, to hold her up in the foyer of her building, in addition to which there were problems at the ad agency: a new boss who didn't like her. Also, her mother had been in a car accident. She decided that she wanted to move to Milwaukee, where she came from, and since I had no great desire to live anywhere other than on Florizona Avenue, which was now impossible, I agreed. It was a heady feeling at last to be able to give her something, after so many years during which, every time we'd gone out for dinner, she'd had to pick up the bill. Not that a little house in Milwaukee was in any way going to compensate for the loss of *this* place—this fantastic place—or for the knowledge that I had failed my mother. And yet it was something: a life. So we moved.

And of course, when I went to Milwaukee, I brought the notebooks with me. And once there, in that funny little brick house of ours, I had no idea whatsoever what to do with them. There was no barbecue pit in *that* backyard. I considered various hiding places—a dormant dumb-waiter and a sort of hidden shelf, way up in the back of one of the closets—before I realized that at this point there was really no longer any need to look for a hiding place. Because of course no one who knew about the notebooks, who knew what they were, and might have recognized them, was anywhere near Milwaukee. And so, taking a page from "The Purloined Letter," I started just leaving them out on my desk. Once Molly strolled in and asked me about them. "Oh, those are the notebooks I wrote poetry in when I was a kid," I said. "I dug them out of the house in Wellspring before we sold it. I thought I'd read them over." And she smiled, and said, "That's nice," and left the room as obliviously as she had entered it. She had a habit, my first wife, of wandering in and out of rooms for no particular reason that I found vexatious.

So now I was a husband and a homeowner, and I had to do something. Molly had found a job with an advertising firm most of the clients of which were big Milwaukee breweries. Our house had cost so little, comparatively speaking, that even after buying it I still had quite a bit of money left from the sale of the big house, my mother's house. I told her that I was going to give myself a year to write a new novel, and that if that didn't pan out, I'd give up writing and get a job, and since it seemed that now I could afford that year, she gave her assent. Now, every morning, I would sit down in front of the computer—I'd bought myself one of the new Macintoshes, which seemed so astonishing at the time, even though these days we would find them ridiculously slow—and gaze at the little simulacrum of a blank page that the screen offered up. Next to me, on top of my desk, sat the notebooks. It wasn't my intention at this point to do anything with them. On the contrary, I only kept them out because I hoped they might bring me luck, inspire me to write the book that Georgiana Sleep (who had in the meantime changed jobs, moving to a bigger, more prestigious house) would actually buy.

And then for two weeks I just sat there. It wasn't that I

didn't have an idea—I did—I just couldn't seem to bring myself to depress the keys. My fingers either felt heavy as iron weights, or they felt gummy and rubbery, or they shook so badly I could barely control them. And every one of those days, that awful virtual blank page stared out at me. I hated it. On old computers, when you wrote, you typed pulsing green letters onto a black screen. Somehow that was easier, because it looked less like writing in a book. The Mac's blank page, because it was more real, was more of a rebuke.

I remember that on one of those afternoons, just after lunch, I suddenly felt, for the first time in days, that I might actually be able to control my fingers. So I hurried to the computer and switched it on. It took an eternity to boot up, and by the time it had, whatever surge of hopefulness or self-confidence had seized me was gone. Still, my fingers worked. I thought, "Try typing. Just typing. To get yourself back in the mood."

And then, more or less on a whim, I typed out the sentence, "To make love in a balloon . . ."

To make love in a balloon . . .

I blinked. I looked at the words in front of me. They looked so good to me on the screen, so fresh and—well—so *real*, that I typed out the second sentence of Boyd's novel, too.

I smiled. This was art. This was fun.

I opened the first notebook. I checked to make sure that I had gotten the sentences down correctly. (I had.) Then I typed out the third sentence—and just went on, until I finished the entire first chapter. And why not? The prose was so good! True, this was typing, not writing—and yet, I reasoned, there was practical benefit to be gained even from that. Because if I ever decided, as Anne had contemplated, to "find" the notebooks and then to try to arrange for their publication, of course it would be necessary to have a presentable typescript. The very copy that Boyd himself, much to his wife's chagrin, had resisted making.

The next several days passed in a trance. I stopped answering the phone. In the evenings I was in such a good mood I think my wife suspected me of doing cocaine. By night I was enthusiastic, appreciative, kind, a superb lover, a terrific cook. I laughed out loud at the television, even at the stupidest sitcoms. We had her parents over for dinner and I charmed them. And then in the mornings I would wake up early, vigorous, alert to the smell of coffee, eager once again to lose myself in *Gonesse*. If typing out the book was better than writing it or reading it, it was because it allowed for a degree of immersion in an alternative and beautiful world the likes of which, in my own work, I'd never before known. Now I understood why Jonah Boyd had grown so remote from me that afternoon at the arroyo! Why concern yourself with reality, when you had this at your disposal—this better, richer realm?

Nor did I merely type. Oh, at first I was strict with myself; I kept myself to the role of scribe. But then as I got deeper into the manuscript, I also got bolder. If I were to find what I considered to be a stylistic infelicity, a misplaced "but," or a repeat of two words within the same paragraph, or (heaven forbid) a dangling modifier, I would make a silent repair. Or if I came to a sentence in which I felt that Boyd had chosen the wrong word or phrase, or brandished a cliché, or if I felt I could come up with a better way of saying whatever it was that needed to be said, I would slip the change in furtively, slyly. Like a shoplifter. The computer made this easy; on a computer screen the labor of rewriting is rendered invisible. One would have had to consult the notebooks themselves to discover any evidence of my tampering. And this chance to clean up, to correct, to improve, to tighten the screws, even on occasion to cut, only amplified the sense of euphoria that had claimed me, much like the one, I see now, that had sometimes claimed my mother when she undertook her massive cleaning details. For by making these changes, I was also putting my mark upon the novel. I was making it, in a small way, my own.

And meanwhile Georgiana called me at least once a week. "Fantastically," I'd say when she asked how things were going—and refuse to say more. She kept begging for clues. I think she could tell from the tone of my voice that I was onto something, into something. "Just a description, some hint of what the novel's about," she'd plead, and I'd laugh, and tell her nothing. In all honesty, it felt good, for once, to have the shoe on the other foot.

Now this is very important, and I hope you believe me: Until the very end it was my intention, if I sent out the typescript at all, to send it out as what it was, Jonah Boyd's lost novel, which I had discovered and completed. But then I reached the last page of the fourth notebook. Now it was time for the most difficult part of the job—completion, the writing of the unwritten last two chapters. Fortunately I remembered everything Boyd had told me, that afternoon at the arroyo. And yet when I settled down to actually do the work, I decided that some of Boyd's plans weren't nearly as smart as he'd believed them to be. In all likelihood, I decided, he would have changed his mind too, once he'd reached that stage. And so instead of adhering strictly to the plan he had laid out for me, I went my own way, and produced, in a matter of days, a pair of chapters that seemed to me in every way worthy of, if not better than, what preceded them, even if at certain key points they diverged from the creator's master plan.

Now comes the hard part. The shameful part. The part for which I fear you will never forgive me.

I printed out and corrected the finished typescript. Then I printed out a fresh copy. Georgiana called. "How's the novel going?" she asked.

"I just finished," I said.

"You finished!" she said. "Then what are you waiting for? I want to see it!"

Believe me or not as you choose, but from the morning I changed the title to *The Sky* and put my name on the title page, to the morning when I handed the package containing the manuscript across the counter at our neighborhood post office, to the morning when Georgiana called to say that not only she but the entirety of her editorial board—that tormenting "we"—had adored my book and that she was preparing to make an offer for it, I thought I was only doing it to teach her a lesson.

And the lesson was this: Because I was me, I was convinced that upon actually reading the novel, Georgiana would decide to use the occasion, once again, to slap me down, put me in my place; that she would either reject the novel out of hand, or suggest that if I made a thousand changes she might reconsider it, and then once I had made them, reject it; and all this despite the distinct note of enthusiasm I had been hearing in her voice. But now, when she slapped me down, at least I would have the satisfaction of knowing at last that the problem was not with my writing; the problem had never been with my writing; on the contrary, the problem was with the system of submissions itself, which was deeply corrupt, and manned by stooges who would lavish praise upon the works of the already famous with the same Pavlovian predictability with which they would disparage and dismiss the works of the hardworking but little known. And having established, once and for all, that all these years of rejection said nothing about me or about my work, then I could quit writing, and be free. I had seen something similar happen in an episode of *The Partridge Family* that I remembered from my childhood, in which Laurie goes to work as a substitute teacher in Danny's class, and because he is her brother, she flunks him on every paper. At last he turns in a story by Hemingway; she still flunks him. He reveals the truth, she is abashed, a lesson is learned.

That was the lesson I wanted to teach Georgiana: She would reject my novel, and I, with glorious composure, would reveal that it was not my novel at all; it was Jonah Boyd's.

Needless to say, the plan had a lot of holes. Indeed, the numerous practical difficulties inherent in it would probably, in the long run, have stopped me from ever putting it into action. (Among other things, I would have had to explain how I had happened upon Jonah Boyd's manuscript in the first place.) Only, as it turned out, I never had to put it into action, because far from responding with diffidence or disdain, Georgiana bought the book, praising me for having overcome "creative hurdles" to become "the writer I was born to be." And the whole time, of course, it wasn't my book at all. Yet how could I tell her that? How could I do otherwise than go along with her, when what she was offering me was the thing I had craved for years, for most of my life, ever since that Thanksgiving when Jonah Boyd had come to visit and awakened in me a sense of possibility to match my ambition? I had meant for her to learn a lesson. Now she turned the tables on me, and proved that all along her responses had been sincere; which meant that all along the problem really *had* been with me, with what I had written. A completely private humiliation was the price I had to pay for at last getting what I'd always wanted.

Well, you know the rest of the story. I signed a contract and was paid some money, which pleased Molly. But then, in the months before the publication, I got cold feet; I worried that someone I had never heard of, some stranger to whom Jonah Boyd might also have read aloud from his notebooks, might read my novel and recognize its origins. Or that you might remember, or Daphne, or Glenn. None of you did, as it happened. Still, I was afraid, and so, under the guise of revision, I set about making a thousand more changes to the manuscript, all toward the goal of disguising it, rendering it unrecognizable even to that theoretical person. That person who, as it turned out, was you.

The Sky came out. It didn't do terribly well, which suited me fine. I didn't want it to circulate too widely. Ironically, even the critics who didn't like it loved the last two chapters. Still, it served its function, because now I had a contract to write a new novel, and on this novel I set to work in earnest. I got a job teaching at a local college. And really, Denny, it was astonishing. Before, writing for me had been an anguished, agonized, slow procedure, marked by fits of amnesia from which I would emerge not remembering a thing about what I had done, and fits of despair from which I would emerge wanting to drink, and long, blank days when the sentences came out in states of arthritic contortion and I wanted to tear my hair out, or hurl the hated Macintosh out the window. Now that

Georgiana had affirmed me, though, I wrote as easily, as fluidly, as Jonah Boyd himself claimed always to have done. The new novel was a joy to write, and perhaps for that reason, a joy to read: It was a huge success.

As for the notebooks, I kept them close by, even though my suspicion was that by bringing me to the point at which I now found myself, they had expended their last gust of magical beneficence. Now they were just leather and paper, paper and leather. They had even lost much of their smell.

Still, I didn't dare throw them out, or burn them. To do so, it seemed to me, would have been to risk some sort of cosmic retribution. Like desecrating a corpse. Aren't there rules about what you can and can't do with talismans? Aren't they indestructible?

The notebooks traveled with me all over the country. Through two marriages, and three houses, until I made my way back here. And really, regaining this house—that was the final proof that the notebooks were magic. That was the final purpose—I thought—of whatever spirit inhabited them, to restore the house my mother had loved into the hands of one of her children. The message seemed clear: I should now inter them forever in the grave that fate had designated to be theirs. And so the very day I signed the deed and took the keys and came back to this house, I returned them to the little sooty chamber from which I had removed them so many years earlier, on the occasion of our dispossession. And there they have stayed until tonight. Now I give them to you.

Ben opened the file drawer at the bottom of the little desk at which Nancy used to sit when she paid her bills. He took out the notebooks.

"Well, now you have it," he said, "The truth. That's what you said you came here for. And you shall also have these."

He pushed them across the table. I didn't touch them.

"They're yours," he went on. "As is my fate. What you do with them—and it—is up to you. Decide, if you want, purely on the basis of what you believe to be right. And yet I can't help but think that there must be *something* that you want." He leaned in toward me. "Come on, what is it? There must be. Otherwise why would you have come?"

"But there isn't," I insisted—and even as I said it, I realized, for the first time, that there was.

It seemed so obvious. So beautifully obvious. What I wanted, and what he alone could give me.

Ben put his hand over mine. It was the first time in our lives he had ever touched me.

"Come on," he said. "Tell me."

So I told him.

Fourteen

R EADER — OH, HOW I have looked forward to writing this sentence, hurrying my way toward it with impatience and eagerness!—reader, I married him.

The house is mine. Ben has died, and rules are rules. It doesn't belong to Daphne. It doesn't belong to Mark. Despite all Nancy's efforts, it has ended up not in the hands of her children, or of her children's children, but of her husband's secretary. The one who loaded the dishwasher wrong. The one forgotten in the will. The house is mine, and there is not a damn thing any of them can do about it.

I sound petulant, which I don't want to. I sound as if it was only for the house that I married him, when in truth there was great love between Ben and me. Hadn't he always longed for the touch of an older woman? I gave it to him, at long last completing the work Anne had started. And Ben—well, despite my lifelong insistence that I would never marry, anyone who ever bothered to look in my linen closet would have found the thirty years worth of back issues of *Modern Bride,* stacked neatly along with the sheets. I didn't subscribe; I bought my porn as furtively as any teenager. And like a teenager, I kept it hidden, a shaming late-night pleasure to be pored over while eating ice cream or ramen noodles, when no one was around to see.

Maybe Ben recognized that behind my lifelong avowal never to marry there lay a secret longing. For when I reminded him of the day we met—that day on which I had accidentally eaten half his sandwich at Minnie's—he said, "Well, doesn't that prove that we were meant for each other, Denny dear? For what was the dividing of that sandwich, if not a foreshadowing of the champagne toast at the wedding, the bride and groom sipping from the same glass?"

It was the sweetest thing any man had ever said to me.

Minnie's, by the way, is gone. In its place on Calibraska Avenue there is now a Ralph Lauren Polo store.

He was diagnosed with a brain tumor only three months after our marriage. By then we had managed to finish furnishing the bedrooms, and were just getting started on the landscaping. His writing block lifted, and he went to work on a new novel. Then one afternoon (and much to my surprise) he asked me if I'd mind giving him piano lessons. Despite being his mother's son in so many ways, until that day Ben had never once touched a piano. And now, for some reason, he wanted to learn. And though I was hardly qualified as a teacher, I did give him lessons, even managing to bring him to the point where he could play a Bach musette through to the end. Of course, by then the headaches had gotten so bad he could barely focus on the score.

Brain cancer runs in families. What killed Ben was the same type of tumor that had killed his mother, and probably (though no one is certain) his great-grandfather—amazing to him, if not to his doctors—and though the intervening years had brought many advances in treatment, none were adequate to save his life. And so I sat by his bedside as I had sat by Nancy's, taking notes while he explained to me how he wanted to end his new book.

That book is now finished. After he died, I spent six months cleaning up the typescript, making minor improvements for consistency, and putting the finishing touches on the last chapters, which were incomplete—all in scrupulous keeping with his instructions. The novel tells, after a fashion, the story of my life—everything he left out of *The Eucalyptus*. I admit, the discovery that he had chosen to narrate it from my point of view startled me at first: Strange to be typing out an account the "I" of which, rather than me, is someone else's *idea* of me, and in which for every moment of astonishing accuracy there is another where "I" am made to do or say something I never did or said. Still, I resisted the impulse to change or correct. Much as when I had been obliged to transform Ernest's incomprehensible notes into coherent English, I looked upon my task as one of ordering, of tying up loose ends. Call it the secretarial impulse, and then decide for yourself how much it differs from the artistic one.

One thing I must admit: Until I read Ben's last novel, I never guessed that both he and Nancy had known all along about my affair with his father. For this shortsightedness, I am ashamed.

A few weeks before his death, Daphne flew down from Portland to stay with us. She left her children and her husband behind. For the duration of her visit she behaved as if nothing had changed since the days when her mother had ruled at 302 Florizona Avenue, as if I was still Denny the secretary, in the kitchen only because Nancy had summoned me to assist in some domestic crisis. Thus when she emerged from her old bedroom in the mornings, the first question out of her lips was usually: "Is there coffee?" She never made any herself, though intermittently she baked cookies, and then left the mess in the sink for me to clean up. Also, she made a silent point of rearranging the dishes in the dishwasher after I had loaded it. And it was my dishwasher! For Ben's sake alone I held my tongue.

I don't know what she fathomed to be at the root of my marriage to her brother—she wouldn't tell me—only that she must have regarded our union as fundamentally bogus, and me as some sort of predatory interloper who had entrapped Ben solely for the purpose of robbing her of her rightful inheritance. Nor did it matter how valiantly Ben tried to dissuade her from this point of view, to convince her that we really did love each other. She clung to her convictions as stubbornly as Nancy would have.

Of course I kept the notebooks hidden. This was as much Ben's choice as mine. He said he never wanted to lay eyes or hands on them again. He said it was why he could write now. And I, for my part, from the day he pushed them to me across the tulip table until the day of his death, kept up my end of the bargain, and made sure that they remained out of his sight as well as his reach. Their safekeeping and concealment were my responsibility, just as it was understood that once Ben died, it would be my decision whether or not to reveal that they had never been lost. Whether or not to ruin him in order to do justice to Jonah Boyd.

That was a hard decision to make, but I have made it at last. Like Anne Boyd, I don't see what good is to be derived from privileging the needs of the dead over those of the living. I am alive. And so I shall prove my loyalty to my husband, and make sure that no one ever finds what he kept hidden all those years in the barbecue pit.

Like his mother, he died at home. At the funeral neither Daphne nor Mark would even look at me. This time they were both staying at the Ritz-Carlton, and when I pressed them to come by the house afterward, they refused. "I just couldn't," Daphne said, squeezing my hand in a way that suggested at least a lingering touch of affection. Mark, on the other hand, turned from me without a word. Cold bastard.

That afternoon I had Ben's colleagues from the English department over, along with some of his students. His students loved him. There was coffee, and pie, and a festive feeling in the house that almost reminded me of Nancy's Thanksgivings, when I was a stray, and none of those students had even been born.

I guess what Daphne and Mark couldn't accept, what they couldn't tolerate, was that even if I'd wanted to, I couldn't have given them that house. Even if Nancy's ghost had come lurching up from the underworld and stuck a red hot poker in my ribs, I couldn't have done it. It was out of my hands.

Yet here is the great irony: A few months after Ben died— and much to the amazement of every resident of Wellspring— the university got a new president, a fiscal liberal who one day very quietly undid the rule that had been the bane of Nancy Wright's life. This means that we owners of houses built on university-owned plots are to be given the option of buying those plots for a dollar—a decree that at once puts an end to an old and contentious policy, and also allows the university to take advantage of some lucrative tax breaks.

Who knows what really lies behind the change, or even how the new president managed it? Perhaps some law professor was planning a clever suit. Perhaps the board of trustees got greedy. In any case, I shall soon be the owner of this land as well as the house on which it sits, and could leave them, if I chose, to Daphne's children. But I think instead that I shall leave them to Susan Boyd's children. That family ought to get something in compensation for the life out of which her father was swindled. So why not this house, where, after all, the crime was planned and committed?

Besides, she is a secretary.

There was only one thing left to do. I finished writing Ben's novel in early November—all but the coda you are reading now. Thanksgiving night was clear and brisk that year, illuminated by a mostly full moon. I had no one over. I ate, by myself, part of a turkey breast, and some potatoes reheated in the microwave. Then around ten I stole out to the barbecue pit. I removed the notebooks from their sooty cache, freed them from their swaddling of plastic and foil. In the middle of the hearth, under the spit, there is a sort of charred black grate meant for holding coals or wood, and on this I arranged the notebooks, along with a cradling of crumpled newspaper. Finally I lit a match, and dropped that in, too.

I am pleased to tell you that Nancy was completely wrong about the chimney—it draws marvelously. In the hearth the leather covers of the notebooks yellowed and lifted and crumpled, revealing for a millisecond a few lines of blue prose. Up and up the smoke rose, a gray-black balloon drifting out toward the Pacific, while with a stick I ground into ashes the body of evidence, the body of the work, the body of Jonah Boyd.

A NOTE ON THE AUTHOR

David Leavitt is the author of several novels, including *The Lost Language of Cranes, While England Sleeps,* and *Equal Affections,* as well as the short story collections *Family Dancing, A Place I've Never Been,* and *The Marble Quilt,* recently brought together as *Collected Stories.* He wrote the Bloomsbury Writer and the City title *Florence: A Delicate Case.* A recipient of fellowships from both the John Simon Guggenheim Foundation and the National Endowment for the Arts, he lives in Gainesville, Florida, and teaches at the University of Florida.

A NOTE ON THE TYPE

The text of this book is set in Linotype Sabon, named after the type founder, Jacques Sabon. It was designed by Jan Tschichold and jointly developed by Linotype, Monotype and Stempel, in response to a need for a typeface to be available in identical form for mechanical hot metal composition and hand composition using foundry type.

Tschichold based his design for Sabon roman on a font engraved by Garamond, and Sabon italic on a font by Granjon. It was first used in 1966 and has proved an enduring modern classic.